Metaphorosis

May 2019

Beautifully made speculative fiction

Also from Metaphorosis Books

Metaphorosis

May 2019

---

edited by
B. Morris Allen

Metaphorosis Books

Neskowin

ISSN: 2573-136X (online)
ISBN: 978-1-64076-139-1 (e-book)
ISBN: 978-1-64076-140-7 (paperback)

Metaphorosis

May 2019

edited by
B. Morris Allen

Metaphorosis Books

Neskowin

ISSN: 2573-136X (online)
ISBN: 978-1-64076-139-1 (e-book)
ISBN: 978-1-64076-140-7 (paperback)

May 2019

Somewhere to be Going

Katrina Smith

The changeling boy goes to space in a ship of his own making. Late at night, as the house sleeps, he labors over steel and circuits in his father's garage. Next to the classic Tesla S and the mid 20th century Cadillac with predatory tailfins, Corbin carves curves into plastic, coaxes lines of electricity until they bloom like branching veins in the structure of his heart's desire.

As dawn begins he steps back to look at the night's work. He isn't good at engineering, physics, or design—to his father's great disappointment and the frustration of his tutors the boy has failed aeronautics more than once, unable to remember the inviolable rules by which humans interact with the universe.

None of that matters now. All night he works by instinct, following the instructions in a song whose notes linger just out of his reach. It's difficult. He doesn't always understand. He is placing a switch up high, higher than he can reach from a sitting position. Whom is he building this for? Static cracks between the connections in his brain.

Days pass as they always have. He walks the earth: learns chemistry, reads poetry, memorizes the names and dates of those who have come before. His lab partner is a girl named Mira with wild, curly hair and dark eyes. She's going to be a doctor on Mars one day and loves space as much as he does. She did not have trouble passing physics, engineering, or design. His best friend Nikolai thinks she is beautiful. Corbin knows she is; her mind is crystalline, focused and perfect, refracting knowledge into something surprising and new. She lives next door but is never home, always in the lab after school. Mostly he just sits and talks while she works. She is thinking about space today, vast coldness and planets made from brilliant gases, quiet as she works on their experiment. Something he says—it's never something he meant to be funny—makes her laughter burst louder even than the static: bright and unexpected as a solar flare, and just as warm on his skin.

After school Corbin plays soccer. He's good at plucking the ball from the sky when it comes towards his goal. He is unmoved by the opposing team's thundering, imminent violence. Usually he and his friends win. Today he's clumsy and slow to act; there is the relentless buzzing in his ears and besides, his joints are aching. There are scouts here from a prestigious university and his best friend Nikolai plays like he's possessed, scoring perfect goal after perfect goal. Each time the team screams in triumph.

But in the sky above them starlings swirl and dance their migratory patterns. They are like one body, a thousand minds becoming one dagger that strikes the horizon and scatters. Instinct calls them to the wind. He feels a hollow aching in his bones. What would a solar wave be like to ride? He makes careless mistakes. He's slow; his body is strangely heavy, as if he is made from mud and wattle and cracking, now, to pieces. He tries to throw his body into the path of the ball below but misses once, twice, a third time. They lose the soccer game. Afterwards, Nikolai runs to Corbin, his face hard, and pushes him with both hands.

The ground is wet and unpleasant and his eye throbs where Nikolai hit it, but it's the force building around Nikolai that Corbin shrinks from. Cold and colorless, this pressure is nothing like Mira's joy. This is an emotion to be endured until it burns all the oxygen in the room. He watches the starlings above Nikolai's screaming face and thinks instead of the gas giants, their frozen atmospheres twisting with their surfaces so that there is no sense of where one ends and the other begins. When the coach pulls Nikolai off him, the migration floods over the curve of the horizon and out of sight. Instead of relief there is a hollowness. Once, Nikolai's anger would have made Corbin upset. Now, none of this matters.

He has dinner that night with his mother and father at the small table in the kitchen instead of the formal dining room. His father is home early for once, the aeronautics firm he runs making do without him. His mother cuts lavender and sunflowers from their walled garden, puts them in a vase, makes the dinner herself—steamed broccoli, a salad, a thin, lean slice of meat. She does this when she feels the need to be particularly maternal. Obviously she spoke to Nikolai's mother after the soccer game.

So, she says. I heard you had a hard day?

Do we need to get you a tutor? his father says.

I told you, she says. About his friend.

They exchange a long look, having forgotten that the boy has outgrown their capacity for public privacy.

His father clears his throat.

I don't care about Nikolai. Everything's fine, Corbin says, thinking instead of gaseous nebulas swirling fuchsia and violet, the color and shape of his parents worry, stars unfurling solar energy into the universe—the truth, now, but of course she thinks he is lying, so he picks up his full plate, the food untouched, and places it gently next to the sink.

Sometimes you outgrow people, Corbin, his father says. Maybe it's better to move on.

Late that night after his mother falls asleep and the light goes out in his father's home office the boy stands in the garage with his craft. He felt the ship calling to him all day, an aching in his core like he'd been kicked. He checks the electrical connections, the components, every line he'd welded. He can feel the milky way cracking open above him, electricity in his bones.

He looks at the ship. He doubts. This is madness. What is he doing? He loves this family. For all their faults, they are more his than anything ever will be again—his mother with her walled garden, his father with his money and his brilliant designs, and he, their son, primed to stretch the future they've worked for out past their own ends. For all their material focus and distractions, for all their staid comfort and practicality, Corbin knows should he call them here—he considers this, the way he knows his voice would quaver, thin and young in the way it sometimes gets still when he is scared—and he should show them the ship and he should say, *I don't know what I did and I need you.* He should fight against this alien itching in his throat, this too-easy stretching towards the stars, the relentless joy at leaving everything behind. The way those he loves have become strangers. The easy way he consigns them all to earth.

But there is also a feeling like stretching after a long sleep. Like the first game on a green field after winter. He wonders if the birds long to stay at the end of summer, when the shadows start to stretch.

How quickly those who stay behind starve.

While he has been thinking, his hands have been moving, checking every inch of his craft, and now they hesitate on a junction that must be filled. He can sense the wrongness of it. What if he has forgotten something important? How will he live, up there in the dark?

When he was small, after he'd made his first minor rocket out of scraps from his dad's home office, they went out to drive in an ancient Cadillac. How his father got the fuel for it, no longer common even when he himself was young, the boy has no idea. It was a rare thing, just the two of them—his mother fussed over the lack of autodrive, the probability of their certain death. Frightened by the growl of the primitive engine, she retreated to the garden to tend her experiments. His father laughed. *What better ride than this for a wonder such as him?* he'd said, and Corbin had hugged

against him, tight, not wanting to let go of
the pride in his father's voice. *You've got
to know the past to change the future,* his
father said. The boy remembers the
chrome gleaming everywhere, seeming
somehow old and new at once, his legs
sticking to the front seat, the carefree way
his father whistled and laughed as he
explained the outdated internal
combustion engine. The boy tilted the
mirror on his door to watch the tailfins
slicing the street behind them, his arm
crooking itself on the open window. He
had never felt safer.

It takes maybe an hour to mount the
tailfins, and then there is nothing left to
build.

He puts his hands on the smooth metal
shell of his ship and pushes it past all his
father's favorite machines to the front of
the garage. He lingers in the dark, warm
comfort of the small shop, tilts his head to
listen to the familiar small sounds of the
house at night. His hands shake a little as
he unlocks the garage door.

But when he rolls his ship, wheels
creaking, into the waiting moonlight,
there's no more doubt. Alien and familiar,
these pieces make a whole that belongs
somewhere else. It's is beautiful,

piecemeal and perfect, crafted from a hundred scavenged pieces—Earth's great diversity on display.

Above him, worlds spin and toss against the black. Somewhere up there are his people. His blood rings in his ears. He looks at the cold vastness of space waiting for him to explore it. The dissonance in his ears eases as he boards the craft. Somehow his arms and legs reach the switches perfectly. He realizes all at once that he has never been more himself than he is now.

The stars are sounding on high. It's almost loud enough to drown out someone calling his name. He looks to the side. His mother and father are there in their pajamas, ludicrously out of place and looking lost. Mira is there too, strangely, and he remembers—the thing that made her laugh was that he told her he had a spaceship of his very own, that he had made it with his own hands. She is crying. It's too late now. It's all too late now. He is sorry, momentarily, for the look on his mother's face. She has loved him. He has been for many years their changeling child, a foundling pulled to earth and into their orbit. This is a good place. He has liked being in a good place.

There is a loud ringing in his ears, a song in his blood, but still there is his mother's face, and it is asking him to stay.

There she is, gentle hands full of violets the way they always are full of some plant or cutting; Dad, awestruck in wonder, not at his son but at the ship his son has built. He is running his hands over each seam, and then he looks up at Corbin, and all the pride crack to pieces, sudden veins of grief filling the spaces between.

You're leaving, he says. He turns to Corbin's mother, holds her tightly, a wordless transmission passing between them. Corbin hears it anyway. *It was hardly any time at all, and now he's gone.*

He could speak. He thinks he remembers how, still. An echoing boom: Somewhere nearby—maybe down in the valley—a bright flash of light burns upwards. Soon another, and then another, the sky filling, the world over, with smoke and flame. He is not the only one. There are others, like him, who have grown here, in the good place, who are hearing the greater universe calling them home. Line after line of light leading the way forward to the unknown. He knows the yearning of the starlings. It's almost unbearable.

While his eyes were tracing the way forward the others have drawn in fire in the sky, his mother has climbed the stepladder he used to get into the craft, the one she used for holiday lights and high places, and he looks down to see her kind, quick hands tucking sprigs of rowan and rue, lavender and thorn, around him. She is smiling and crying, sad and joyful both at once.

"Go," she says, and there is the feeling of a dam breaking—something righted and destroyed at once. His father helps her climb down, and he watches the way they lean on one another as they stand on the dew-soaked earth. He hopes never to forget it.

When they move far enough away for safety, he fires up the rockets. Their faces hang, pale smears on the dark ground below, until nothing but the stars are in his eyes.

It takes only moments to break the atmosphere, but the scent of herbs lingers, scenting the night, long after he leaves the earth.

See Katrina Smith's story "Somewhere to be Going" online at Metaphorosis.
If you liked it, leave a comment. Authors love that!
Remember to subscribe to our e-mail updates so you'll know when new stories are posted.

About the story

I have an obsession with birds who leave their young to be fostered by different species, and I have a fifteen year old son. Over the years, he's given me motivation when I've needed it and been my biggest fan. I've written him a short story for his birthday nearly every year since he learned to read. Sometimes these are first drafts that go nowhere, but he loves them anyway because, well, I'm his mom and it's a one-of-a-kind present. Sometimes they do go somewhere interesting, like this one did.

This birthday, I thought about how it won't be very long at all before he's heading off into the greater world — exploring his own universe. How I have the pleasure of watching him take parts of the life his dad and I have built, whether that means hobbies or mannerisms we share or a way of looking at and interacting with the world, and put his own spin on it so that these familiar things become something completely new and uniquely his, not ours anymore. And teenagers, well — I'm not saying anything new, but they can go from being the familiar being you love to complete strangers and back again so fast you'll get whiplash trying to keep up.

Watching him interact with the wider world and grow into himself has been bittersweet in a way I didn't anticipate. So I wrote him this story, about a boy who leaves a family who loves and the rightness of that, how it's a natural step all young take when they leave the nest. And because I am who I am, and I love cuckoo birds, spaceships, the old, dangerous stories of fae changelings, and my son, who is about to embark on his own journey into the unknown, it couldn't hardly be a typical story about coming of age. Instead, it ended up being about a changeling boy who is much loved by his parents, but who follows the natural sounding of instinct and builds a spaceship to explore the stars.

A question for the author

Q: Do you use critique groups or other resources to polish your writing?

A: I've experienced a lot of different critique arrangements over time. When I was an undergrad, I started getting a group of people whose work I admired together outside of class to read, write and encourage each other with feedback for each others' work. I have an MFA in Fiction from George Mason University, so I've also experienced a few dynamics when it comes to critiquing and being critiqued by mentors, professors, classmates and peers. I'm thankful for all of those experiences, because they really taught me how to take constructive criticism, disconnect the personal from the work, and offer clear, concise feedback in return. I'm not entirely comfortable with having twenty or thirty people involved in the early stages of a draft, though. It can be too much to synthesize when you have that many opinions to go through.

Now, I have a group of 3-4 people I tend to run work by for feedback once I get a first draft finished. These are people I've met at some point during my writing journey, either when I was getting my degree or from interactions in writing communities and retreats, and who write a diverse set of things. I've actually found it's really helpful to have someone who doesn't normally read or write speculative fiction take a look at a draft — they'll see things that reviewers who are familiar with SF/F won't, and often what they respond to is surprising. So I tend to send things to a few people I trust, and then see where the areas of overlap are when I move to editing.

I also love reading and responding to work, too. Reciprocating feedback is exciting. It helps me feel intimately connected to my personal writing community and recharges me on days when I'm having a hard time interacting with my own stories.

About the author

Katrina Smith reads and writes speculative fiction by the side of a green river in Bend, Oregon. She holds an MFA from George Mason University.

@allwaysmyways

One for the Wounded

Phoenix Alexander

"Minutes... they are the easiest to kill," he whispered. His voice was thick with the drowsiness of spent passion; I thought he had fallen asleep, and felt grateful that he was staying awake with me a little longer. "You need something sharp... Cut their throats. Hit them on the head. Hard and accurate. Break their necks."

I remember thinking that it was an odd thing for him to talk about, this killing. So I lay quite still, on my back, focusing on the cloud of diamonds that was the chandelier above the bed. I had just been made love to for the first time.

I was seventeen years old.

"They are quick, the minutes especially. They like a game... they run through the halls of palazzi, excited by the chase... A little like you, zucchero."

I remember thinking that this saccharine description did not sound like me at all.

"But you haven't really killed people," I said, rolling to my side and pressing against his body. I studied his face for an answer. His eyes were closed, his muscled chest rising and falling. He did not look peaceful.

"Not people. Their time."

"How?"

He sat up suddenly, pushing the sheets aside.

"You talk too much, boy."

"I'm sorry! I'm sorry... please stay." The thought of him leaving was intolerable. I felt stupid; I felt vulgar; I had ruined the enchantment of our evening.

Half-dressed, he turned to face me. His legs stood thick in velvet stockings, his shirt an extravagance in silk over his torso.

"How old do you think I am?"

"...Thirty?"

He laughed and fastened his shirt, his hands moving swiftly and with practice.

"Ninety. I am ninety years old."

I didn't know what to say to that. So I said nothing.

He turned again and looked at me, staying very still. I felt stripped soul-deep by his gaze – but there was nothing lascivious in it anymore. It was a searching so hungry it made me draw the sheets to cover my naked form. I did not know what he wanted. I did not know anything.

If there are words to capture the meaning in his exhalation – the exhaustion, the disappointment – I do not know them. I remember feeling like a stone in the wake of it: the smallest, most unlovely thing. I had done something wrong or failed to do something entirely.

"You never give it back to me," he whispered. "None of you do."

"Give what back?"

I could see the effort of him thinking, trying to define. His fingers made claws and he raised his arms, finally drawing a ragged shape in the air that outlined my form. I sat up, the covers falling down to my waist.

"Would you like to dine with me this evening?" My words came in a rush, and kept coming. Anything to make him stay.

"Shall we walk again by the canal? Will you see the operetta with me tonight?"

I listed all the things we had been doing together the last few weeks of that summer – the best, then, of my young life.

"I don't want that." He spoke the words as if imparting news of a death. I understood, young and naïve as I was. I understood then.

"Will I see you again?" I asked, already knowing the answer.

He did not look at me. "No."

He was inspecting himself in the mirror that stood beside the bed. We were in a hotel I could never afford. He would not have me in his home. I did not even know where in the city he lived.

"It's a terrible thing to be old," he said.

"You look beautiful." I whispered. "You do not look old."

"But I am, I am, I *am*."

He whirled to me suddenly, gripping my face with one hand.

"I have stolen years with my work, you fool! Look into my *eyes*."

I did. I remember seeing something bitter, a world of bitterness that was him and that pulled in everyone he loved or tried to. There was something broken and cold and monstrous in his expression.

"I'm being a teacher to you, boy. I am being the teacher that I never had."

He released me. The pressure of his grip warmed my cheeks; in a horrid way, I missed the contact as soon as it was severed. He pulled a bottle from an inside pocket of his jacket. I saw an idea, vividly, alight in him. A brutal smile broke his features.

"Do you want revenge? Do you want something for the pain I have caused you? For the pain others will cause you? Take this." He held out a small, tear-shaped glass vial. It held a few thimblefuls of a bilious green liquid.

I see that now as the moment where my destiny forked, where I could have taken one path or the other – or perhaps it only seems that way, looking back after all these years. Perhaps I am deluded. Perhaps there was never any choice at all. "Take it," he told me, pushing it into my palm. I could not meet his gaze; there was something shameful in this taking. "Now, I am only going to say this once so listen carefully. That is *acida notte*" – he raised a hand at my exclamation – "...yes, the philter of legend. And yes it is true. Look at my face. It is true." Silence hardened for an awful moment between us. "This is how you use it... and this is how you synthesize it."

When he was through explaining, I wept into my hands. None of it seemed real, or like it *could* be real. It was too terrible.

"I have given you the final ingredient for the philter: pain. The bitterness of the memory of this day. Keep it in your heart: turn it into power. It is how people like us survive. I will be your wound, my boy. Keep me close."

Morning bled yellow in the sky beyond the window. He left.

I tried to look for him. I roamed the city, asking at the places we had visited, and was turned away with scorn and anger. Theaters, cafés, places filled with people worthier than I – an orphan, or at least that was how I like to imagine myself. My family were far away and had not wanted me. I had no-one – and so I clung fiercely to the men I courted. I just needed one relationship that lasted. One would be enough: something in which I could be held, consumed in love, never having to worry about loneliness again. Something to prove *him*, my wound, wrong. That I was not unlovable. That I was worthy of being held. A lover who would say *yes, you are mine and mine alone, and I and yours alone, and I will stay*.

I learned from my first that they never stayed.

On my twentieth birthday – three years after I met him – I used the philter. It was for a small, petty job: a disgraced husband wanted to age his rival a few years. So I did it. It was confusing at first. Frightening. I fell as if in a stupor, waking to a glittering and unfamiliar realm: the place where the time lived. I learned that my lover had been right: minutes were the easiest to kill, because they were small, and fragile. When the philter wore off, I was pulled back into the physical realm gasping, exultant, soaked in my own sweat. And the target I had killed the years from had aged that many years, instantly.

I enjoyed the killing. And I was good at it.

I took years from others, and their years sloughed off me; at the age of twenty-five, my body was smooth and slender, with the faintest beds of muscles on my long limbs. My legs were fast; my eyes keen. I aged another ten years – and my body stayed the same.

Years were the most common prey, and troublesome at first. They were giants in the temporal realm: usually twice the height of a man, sometimes more, sometimes less, and while slow, they were hardy. I found new ways to kill them, with bombs and knives and poisons.

A year from a hated father-in-law.

A spinster who had destroyed the dreams of her student, and from whom I took two years.

Even a wealthy schoolboy, bitter, who stole some of his parent's gold and paid me to age a hated schoolmate five years. I remember the screams of the boy's parents when they woke to find an adolescent in their child's bed; I did not stay to watch the consequences.

In time, I forgot my real age. I saw society pass before my eyes and I enjoyed the watching. I traveled through the world as a ghost. I saw buildings rise and fall, the styles subtly changing. I changed my dress to match the latest fashions. Now silk, now velvet, then back to silk: cloaks, gloves, stockings, tunics. I revolved in a glittering world of my own, my only reality. I made and remade the philter with the horrible ingredients *he* had told me the secret of all those years ago. I became an alchemist, a *profumiere*, a *cavaliere*. An assassin of time.

And each time I worked, each time I drank the philter, I saw his face from that night when I was seventeen: the sweat on his chest making the skin shine, and dead worlds behind his eyes as he told me no, he would not stay.

Looking at this profession with a stranger's eye, one might think it a fair, even attractive prospect: gaining time for ourselves by taking that of others, like a kind of *vampiro*. But the opposite is true. It gives us more years to be tortured by the bitterness that led us along this path. It builds a great hall for the monsters of our regret. I held bitterness close in my heart, like he told me. I made my wound my identity and loved it as fiercely as I could bear.

The parchment in my hand – kissed with the red wax of the Marchesa's seal, flush

with the rose tones of her favored scent –
would have me kill five years from her
husband, Marchese Federico Di Lasciare.
It was a large quarry, one of the largest I
had ever been commissioned to hunt. The
script was harsh and ran ragged on the
page, as if written in fury or after an
excess of wine. *Come to the Palazzo
Lasciare at sunfall*, the note read. *I will be
in the mezzo ballroom on the second floor.*

I dressed in my finest: a tunic
embroidered with spun gold, lambskin
boots, my head aureoled with a silk hood
the edges of which were traced with tiny
black diamonds. I left in the drowsing part
of the day, when the city rested through
the warm hours between luncheon and
the bustle of afternoon.

A towering, curved thing with the
sheen of clean bone, the Palazzo was
organized around a central rotunda
girdled by balustrades and curving forms
of cherubic flesh carved from the purest
marble. Columns reared like gods around
me as I ascended the steps of the
entrance.

The place was quiet, the air heavy and
languid. As I ascended the first stairwell,
the floors became quieter still, as if the

building swallowed sound from its topmost reaches.

I found my client in a cavernous ballroom on the upper floor, as she had said I would. Her scent announced her presence before I saw her. The air was garlanded with heady notes of rose and fuschia, and something else, something sharper, less honeyed but all the more alluring for it. She stood before a fresco of a woman lamenting on the shores of a verdant island. Shimmering threads, picked out in gold leaf, curled around the pearlescent skin of the painted figure; the aspect was upraised in an anguish captured with fierce, sanguine strokes.

"The sorceress who was no sorceress, who made the mistake of thinking that her love could halt the fading of a man's desire."

She turned at the sound of my voice.

A delicate-looking doll of a woman, there was a sadness to the Marchesa that I recognized all too well. Her flesh was pale amber against the fuchsia of her gown. Her cheeks though, were flushed, her pupils wide and black. She held a crystal goblet in each hand.

"She should never have loved him, then? The hero who slew the beast in the labyrinth?" The syllables of her speech fell in odd, wavering patterns.

"No. She should have let him stay lost forever and starve in the dark, adding his bones to those of the men who came before him."

"Your *profumo* is exquisite, Marchesa."

"It is my own creation," she said and withdrew from me, unsteady on her feet. "I would see who I am employing." I swept back my hood with both hands, the diamonds tinkling. She cackled, and there was fear in the sound. "You are a boy, a whelp. How old are you?"

"I am sixty years old," I lied. I was probably older. The truth was that I had stopped caring.

The Marchesa's eyes met mine, finally focusing. Her expression gave nothing away – yet the goblets wavered in her hands for the slightest moment.

"It is true, then," she said finally. "Your profession robs you of years."

Yes: my skin was smooth and unlined, my eyes clear green, the downy beginnings of a beard curving beneath my rounded jaw. Disoriented, she looked from one drink to the other. "Here," she said, finally handing me the one most full. "Saluti." She raised her goblet.

"Saluti." I sipped the wine, watching her over the rim. She drank deep, tilting her head back. "This is good." The wine had notes of chocolate and, again, something bitter; my mouth was warm with the aftertaste.

"Thank you. I added a philter of my own to supplement the flavor." She wiped moisture from her lips with her fingertips. "I suppose I should introduce myself. My name is -"

"Why five years?" I said.

She paused; she looked suddenly young in her uncertainty, the anger ebbing for the briefest moment.

"Because he has wasted half a decade of my life – my best years! – and he must suffer the same fate. My so-called husband." She threw back her head and laughed, unsteady on her feet. "I have my *profumi*. I have my philters. I try to make the most of the days. But I have not known love."

I tried to recall what I had heard about the Marchesa and Marchese di Lasciare. A handsome general, decorated in the war, had brought home a woman from abroad: a rare beauty who was the model of grace in all matters of culture. I hadn't cared to remember any other details. People, to me, were the contents of their mansions in the temporal realm: crystalline structures housing the time left to every living soul, and populated with denizens as strange and frightening as the kaleidoscope of human experience itself. They were nothing else.

With a start I realized that she was still speaking. "You do realize," I interrupted, "that it is a trauma for the body of the victim to take so much time. When I kill five years in the temporal realm, he will age five years in the physical realm – this one – instantly." I snapped my fingers for effect, taking another sip of wine as I watched her expression open in anxiety. It was a cruel joke that the reverse process – the gaining of years – was an equally rapid regeneration, but not a fatal one.

"He has... I know he is different. I always knew. But this last trip he returned with... boys. Young men. He brought them into our home. Into *my* home!" Her accent grew thicker as she raised her voice in a shout. "He has made a fool of me in front of everyone. It is too much. He must pay. And then I can leave."

She turned away, the movement of her gown agitating a sickly-sweet breeze.

"Will you take the job or not?" she said finally.

I drank, considering.

"When?" I murmured.

"Tomorrow night. There will be a ball."

I thought of the years this would take from me. If I succeeded, I would be young, a youth. But the payment would be worth it. It would be a rebirth perhaps, a new beginning... I almost laughed at myself for indulging in such reverie. Of course, nothing would change. I would still be unlovable, inside, but in a younger body, and that would be the only difference. I would still kill the time of others. And I would be wealthy beyond anything I had ever known.

I raised the glass.

"Tomorrow night," I confirmed.

We were on a mezzanine above the ballroom floor, the Marchese and I. People thronged in the rotunda below: nobles from all over the city. The Marchesa moved among the crowd, laughing too loudly at their pleasantries, her hands shaking as she clashed glasses in toast after toast and other such sycophantry. She did not look at us once.

I had kept my silk hood, but now I wore a floor-length, brocaded tunic, my legs supple and lithe in lavender stockings and black leather boots, the heels just tall enough to be elegant, yet not so extravagant as to hamper my mobility. Over my left thumb curled a spike made from shining silver, and in its tip was the drop of *acida notte* I would use to mark my target.

"Exquisite," the Marchese said, circling me. "Absolutely exquisite."

He extended a hand.

I took it, locking my eyes on his.

I saw *him* in his eyes. He looked just as my first lover had looked, the one who used me and left me all those years ago: beautiful beyond words, something in his physicality that made me feel safe, even as his eyes were alive with lust and his mouth twisted into a half-smirk. These kinds of men knew their beauty and wielded it for a weapon. I pitied the Marchesa. I felt his breath on my cheek – and in that moment of distraction I pressed the tip of my thumb spike into the back of his hand, wasp-quick. My fingers fumbled, the skin slick with sweat, and he noticed.

He made an exclamation of surprise and withdrew.

"I do apologize, my lord, I do apologize..." I crooned, stretching out the sounds of my words in obeisance, bowing and pressing my golden hair to his hand so that he would not see the flush of my face. He forgave me laughingly, as I had known he would. Not that it mattered. He clasped my hands and pulled me close.

"What is your name, my beauty?"

"Scarmiglione."

He cocked his head, the expression making him look like a boy.

"Such an old-fashioned name for one so young! Where did you..."

Then he realized. He looked at the scarlet bead of blood on the back of his hand and looked back to me, and knew in that moment exactly who and what I was.

He kept his poise. I will say that. But his flesh lightened, the movements of his fingers controlled and taut.

"Dance with me," he said suddenly.

I could not refuse before the crowd waiting below.

Licking the blood from his skin, he pulled me into him with fierce force, feeling the vial – and every dagger, every weapon, every brute instrument of death – tucked into the folds and hidden pockets of the fabric. I did not care. I smirked into his face, wanting to see the fear in his face, to drink it in. I wanted him to *know* what I was about to do to him. This was a revenge for me as well as the Marchesa. For the youth I had been at seventeen. For the things that had been taken from me and the ugliness that had been left in their place. I had figured out the world in all these years I had stolen. I understood the lie of love.

We descended the stairs, arm in arm, to enthusiastic applause. The musicians saw us come together and struck up a steady waltz. The crowd parted, and faint, tipsy laughter followed us. Federico led me out onto the floor.

His face so close was truly breathtaking. There was no accusation in his eyes, only sadness. He murmured against my ear.

"I deserve this, I suppose. I have wasted years of her life. I owe her some of mine." He turned me sharply and for a moment I almost lost my balance. But he maneuvered our bodies, parallel, into a diagonal, and I am old, and I knew the steps. We dipped and rose in promenade. The music swelled. We slowed at the foot of the grand stairwell amid uncertain applause from the nobles, and he turned me once more.

I could not resist. My taunt hissed, intimate, into his ear.

"I am what happens when you drink people like the wine you piss out when the night is done."

"I accept it," he whispered back. "I accept it."

"You cannot accept it, because you do not know. But you will. You will."

A sob broke my words; I was surprised by tears. No. I would not give him this. How many times had I cried because of men like him? No more, now. No more. I pushed it all down, pushed everything down. I needed to get away from him.

The music yet soared. He moved me in a circle, lowering me so that my hood almost brushed the floor – and then whipped me back to him as the dance ended. The crowd applauded. Our chests rose and fell, our hearts inches apart.

"All I wanted was love," he said sadly. "Promise me one thing. The years you take from me... spend them well."

Love.

The word was a lie I had heard from the lips of countless men before, yet from the Marchese it was almost blasphemy. A man who lived the lie he did – choosing a woman and then exercising every whim of his true nature in private, with men as young as I had been – had no business talking of love.

How had the Marchesa described them? His 'boys?' Creatures innocent of their beauty; perhaps the boys enjoyed it, flaunted it as I had when I was truly, *naturally* young, as if that flaunting and the pleasure they promised would prevent them from being doomed to lovelessness. They would be consumed like sugared confections. It was only a matter of time before their novelty would wear off, and they would be rendered unlovely in the eyes of the world. As I had been consumed. Now I was the sickness that followed the consuming; the knife in the guts that twisted and twisted until the body bent double, trying to crush it out.

Finally free from Federico's terrible embrace, I hurried upstairs and found the space that had been arranged for me by the Marchesa: her private wardrobe. I locked the doors and lay down on the floor among the dresses. With shaking hands I slid the vial of *acida notte* from my breast pocket. My weapons weighed uncomfortably on my body, but they would not for long – because in a moment there would be no body at all.

Looking up at a constellation of gold stars picked out in the turquoise of the Marchesa's dressing room ceiling, I uncorked the bottle and, drinking deep, opened the abyss and beckoned to my demons from the threshold. The soul was stubborn in the body and had to be shaken out by the horrors of the past: horrors that the philter unleashed from their marble prisons in the mind. One horror was most potent of all: the final ingredient of *acida notte*, unique to each one of us who does this work. Our wounds. Our special hatreds, a specific suffering as unique to us as the chemicals of our blood.

I drank, and the horror came.

The lies

The safety in the way that he said he accepted everything I was, and would protect me, and would stay with me

Let me in, one night after weeks of shy circling like skylarks, let me in, purring words in my ears wetted with saliva, just let me

And I did

I couldn't not

Who would not

And it was wonderful

And I forgot the crying of my mother and the livid words of my father, the way he turned his back when he felt anything strongly, as if we could not feel the emotion reverberating from him like a drumbeat

And I forgot the strange looks and cruel names which are just words, just words, and the walls I built around my heart and around myself and the strength of my muscles and the swiftness of my limbs – and the pride that I could outrun any threat, that I could escape from anything if I had to –

And then the meeting him

And the hope

The hope most of all

And the realization that my feet were hurting, and my body was tired. And that I could stop running.

I know now that you never stop running. You run and you run and you never stop for anyone. No matter how good it feels. No matter how safe it seems, and how tired you are.

You keep running. To the end of life itself.

If you watched me you would see my body convulse, my face suddenly not so youthful, the flesh pallid. You would see me jerk like a marionette in the sumptuous fabrics of my costume.

There would be a murmur of air – a flickering – before I disappeared entirely.

Then you would watch me fly.

The curtain of the corporeal world rose to reveal the grand stage beneath it all, folded into the fibers of everything: the temporal realm, the time woven into the spans of our lives. I have taken *acida notte* many times and the sensation is always breath-stealing. Arms flung wide, I soared over a city above a city, an endless metropolis that stretched to each of the compass points around me. A mansion for every life, and a million lives. Each one looked the same from the outside: a tapering cone like a termite's nest, glittering crystalline. Yet inside… inside was were the monsters dwelled.

The Marchese had been marked with the philter I had scratched into him, and so I saw his temporal mansion glowing the green of *acida notte*, like a beacon against lurid sky. None of the others glowed; the few of us who could do this work moved far from each other, for we were lonely and uneasy companions.

Only I hunted this night.

I flew between spires, my body luminous with the white light that pulsed from them. I arced downward, slowly spiraling. Alighting gracefully – my limbs practiced, my body used to adapting to the giddying transition from the earthly to the temporal realms, I headed for the door. Every entrance was the same in this realm: an ivory arch, featureless.

Inside, the mansion was the treacherous quiet of revelry silenced moments before. Secrets – lies – shaped

the Marchese's life and lies, too,
structured the crystal structure of his
temporal mansion. Towering, golden
doors, all shut, made a ring around a
central rotunda. My feet passed silent over
a floor mosaicked with the forms of pink-
skinned youths, bathing and reclining in
scenes of decadence rendered crude in
stone.

This was his idea of love. Of intimacy.
Flesh and flesh.

The place was silent. Pretending to be
uninhabited. Light flickered dimly from
candelabra that hung from the ceiling; the
walls of the mansion glowed a faint green,
bilious with *acida notte*.

A stairwell curved shell-like up one
side of the room, disappearing into
heights obscured by darkness. I ascended.
On the second floor, the architecture of
the mansion changed, breaking the laws
of science that structured the physical
realm. I found myself in a long, carpeted
landing lit by flickering sconces set at
equal distances. More doors stood on
either side of the corridor, golden and
sealed shut. Low moans – muffled cries of
what could have been pleasure or pain –
thickened the air. The floor felt full with
the presences of others as yet unseen.

The doors were not sealed as carefully as the ones in the lower floor. The dross of the Marchese's life could only be hidden so well – and nothing could be hidden from me here for long. I dropped into a crouch and withdrew two curved daggers from the lining of my cloak. If I were quick, I would cut the throats of any temporal beings that tried to stop me. Hugging the shadows of the wall, I padded to the first of the great doors. This one was open a crack; light flickered on the crimson carpet. I brought my eye to the gap and peered into the room.

I was met with a scene of such decadence, such ecstasy, that to witness it felt like a profound violation. Most of the forms in the room were hours – small man-sized creatures, human-appearing – and Federico's were all male. I watched the straining forms of two, three, five individuals (their limbs curled into each other in ways that would not have been possible in the physical realm) upon a gigantic bed, sumptuous clothing making a crazed tapestry on the floor. Movement drew my eye higher; a cloud of seconds cheered and sang, buzzing against the domed ceiling of the room in a living canopy of gold. They appeared as naked, fairy-like creatures, vulgar-faced and delicate-winged. They, too, were male. *Pop pop pop*: the cries of their vanishing were met with the cries of desire from Federico's hours as his lifespan shortened naturally. Second by second.

I moved away, sickened.

I needed to kill five years and leave as soon as I could. There was no enjoyment here; I had the claustrophobic sensation of being trapped in the consuming dark of a giant's stomach. I felt soiled.

I hurried down the corridor. Nothing impeded my path. The temporal beings were preoccupied with their disgusting, endless revelry, or else were hiding. My destination was the upper floors: where the larger temporal beings dwelled.

I was hunting.

The doors stopped appearing, as did the wall sconces, and I found myself walking in near darkness. A few steps more and the darkness grew complete.

I stopped, looking around me, every sense focused. One had to expect anything in this realm. The darkness seemed to grey some distance before me, and slightly higher. The architecture of this place revealed the Marchese's character: pomp and glory shown to the

world on the entrance floor, and the
sordid, hidden things kept locked away up
high, but always there, madmen in the
attic of a palazzo, clamoring and hollering
in their abjection. The Marchese was a
thing that pretended it was beautiful and
that would not harm, would not kill. I
moved slowly forward, quieting my breath
until it was a low, warm hiss that only I
could hear. My blood ran hot and fast in
my veins. I felt control.

My foot found the edge of a step and I
ascended, arms stretched out for balance.
As I moved higher, the light grew grayer
and I began to pick out forms around me:
wide steps of marble, the walls so distant I
could not even see them. The space was
vast. My blood quickened, my breath
rasping now. There was a nakedness – a
vulnerability – I felt here, and I cursed the
Marchese all over again. The space
around me changed. I felt watched.

This was the feeling of brazen, eye-wide
scrutiny that a beautiful person walking
into a room feels.

This was desire that wasn't even
deigned to be disguised: an *I want* as
transient, as shallow, as the hot jet of
climax.

This was a stripping of their personhood, humanity, intelligence, mind, soul, to the shape of their lips and the colors of the eyes and the forms of their hanging limbs and the curves and creases of their sex that was forgotten the instant pleasure had been gained.

This very place was like a shrine to *him*, my first. My wound. It was a sanctuary for the sinful, and a torment for the wounded.

I was exposed. I was unsafe. For all my weapons, my body, my ability – I was vulnerable. I hated the Marchese even more for making me feel like this.

Abruptly, the stairs stopped. I stood on a blinding white plain of marble before a cathedralesque doorway of carved wood. As I peered at the curved forms of its surface, it creaked open, the sound painful and harsh, amplified by space.

"Come," a voice rumbled. "Come."

My gloves gripped the daggers tighter, and I stepped through the door. The light was stark here; starlight glittered through green-glass walls. A faint vein of incense wound through the air. I could not see the ceiling.

Five beds had been arranged in the center of a ballroom a hundredfold as vast and opulent as the real-world ballroom of the Palazzo di Lasciare. White, clean sheets had been folded carefully upon them; white, bone-like spires of wood reared from the four corners of each bed.

Upon each bed lay a year.

Like all of the Marchese's temporal beings, these too, appeared as male. Eyes closed, pale-skinned, they stretched out twice the height of a normal man. They looked serene, dressed identically in white gowns that perversely resembled the garb of the padres that swung censers in the ceremonies of our religion.

The voice spoke again, sonorous, and I almost leapt into the air. My eyes had been so focused on the beds that I had not noticed that around the room stood dozens more years: tall, gowned like the ones lying prostrate – and very much alive. One stepped forward.

"The assassin Scarmiglione. We have been expecting you."

The year who spoke was a giant version of the real-world Federico. Physicality was exaggerated here: his eyes were too green, the curves of muscles beneath his robes unreal in their proportion. He, too, was a lie. The other years looked much the same – such was the Marchese's narcissism! –

but this one was evidently the spokesperson for whatever this was meant to be. "Five years, as promised," he boomed, gesturing to the beds. "Fulfill your mission, *cavaliere*."

I looked from him to the beds. The years there had not moved. Their throats, thick with the apple of the male sex, lay upturned, almost porcelain in the light.

This was too easy.

"They will not resist," the standing year spoke again. "You will not be attacked. This is no trick. You are safe."

I looked from them, to him, to the years around the room. I counted them: twenty-five. The Marchese did not have a naturally long lifespan – but, more importantly, there were not so many that I would be overwhelmed.

No. They did not deserve this peace. He would not control me like this. I would kill the years I chose; it made no difference, but I would be the one to do the choosing. I would be in control; I would not give the Marchese the satisfaction of doing this on his terms.

I raced to the nearest standing year, the marble floor seeming an impossibly vast distance. None of them moved. They looked down on me with something like pity – and the pity kindled my rage.

You use me

You use men like me

And then you look upon us with the fawning eyes of pity as if all of this were our weakness, our fault –

I leapt into the air, the daggers cutting an arc above my head, and buried the blades in the midriff of the year. As my body was pulled back to the ground, I opened a trail in him, tearing the fabric and expanse of his skin alike. There was no blood, no viscera. There was a faint sound of something like pain – and then the creature was gone. I hit the ground, panting, spinning on my feet and tensing in anticipation of retaliation.

Yet the remaining years stood in that infuriating calm, their backs still to the wall. A year pushed himself upright from one of the beds, stretching, and paced over to join his brethren.

"As you wish," said the Federico-year, gazing at me sadly. "That is the first year."

I thrust my daggers back into their sheaths – my hands shaking, so that it took several attempts – and I drew a cudgel from my belt and sprinted over to one of the years still lying on the beds.

The years flinched, looking to one another in unease. This would be no easy death. This was battering, pulping death. I would show them all the ways that a person could be maimed. Drawing tall, enjoying the feeling of my body over the form of the other – I glared at each and every one of the standing years as I raised the cudgel. My gaze locked onto the Federico-year – and I did not look away as I beat out the head of the year on the bed below me. A sigh, a movement of air, a murmuration of fabric, and he, too, was gone.

"Very good," murmured the Federico-year. His expression had hardened, and I felt a delicious satisfaction.

The crystalline walls of the temporal mansion flickered. My vision lightened and I swayed on my feet. The *acida notte* was wearing off; I did not have much time left.

I replaced the cudgel. From a pocket in my tunic I withdrew a bomb. Fury winged me: I was anger-bright, the muscles of my body never feeling so strong, and taken by a frenzy to see all the ways I could make the years suffer.

I heard the collective gasp of the years watching me. They seemed to shrink together: skeletal, serpentine giants whose white flesh and white clothing pushed into one another to make a formless mass. A living barrier that reared suddenly, threatening. Danger, exposed, electrified the room. The Federico-year raised his arm.

"It is not precise. You will kill too many of us. Please stop..."

I activated the explosive mechanism of the sphere, winding the gears in an order that only I knew. The metal clucked in my hands, the machinery whirring. The remaining years on the three beds sat up.

I had never spoken to any of the denizens of the temporal mansions in all the years I had been doing this work. To do so was a swift flight to insanity. But I spoke now.

"For all the men and women whose time you wasted. For all the people you hurt... for me... for *me*..."

I could not finish. My hands shook.

The beds below me seemed to hold the form of my innocence, the one taken from me. My wound.

Keep me with you forever.

I had been careful; I had been good at my work. But I could not be here.

It felt good to relinquish control. I was tired. I was tired of it all, and wanted the fire. I would destroy it all.

As one, the years around the room rushed towards me. All calm had gone from their faces. Open murder was there instead. Countless fingers made claws upon outstretched arms, the fabric of their gowns billowing around them like wings. A ragged white whirlwind of monstrous birds alighted around me, the years on the bed falling over each other as they, too, lunged at me.

I dropped the bomb and raced backwards, my boots almost slipping on the treacherous floor. I almost reached the door – and then the whole world caught fire. There was a detonation behind me that scorched the fabric from my back and hurled me forward. A cacophony of screams – low, high, animal, masculine – deafened my ears. Wood and stone and skin splintered, making diamond dust in the unreality of the mansion. The walls broke.

I pushed myself to my feet, turning to witness the terrible howling of the scorched years on the beds as they boiled in a storm of wood and charred ribbons of fabric; the furnishings caught like dry grass. I had made a conflagration. The impact of the explosions hurled the Marchese-year against one of his companions; licks and sparks of fire took them, too, and the fire whirled triumphant.

How easy it is to ruin something beautiful.

The stairs that had led the way to here, this topmost floor, cracked, crumbling beneath me. I fell – was *pulled* -through the air. My physical body called and ached for me with the force of a whole world. I turned onto my back as air roared around me and I saw a final scene that was luminous in its horror: the giant years in pieces, dismembered, blackening in flames which licked and leapt from one to the other, drinking hair and skin as greedily as the lust that had driven the living man. Years severed clean in half yet still mewling and wriggling as they clung to life. The Marchese-year howling, aflame, clutching at the blasted head of another year, skin crusting like ash, a lifespan reduced to black powder. Thunder beat the air behind me. Smoke and noise. Fire and fury. A ruinous path, as my own life had been ruined. *My wound.*

Bringing arms up to my face, crossing them for protection, I smashed through the crystal stairs and down into the dreaming night, falling beneath stars.

I closed my eyes as the ground flickered, dimmed. My form shimmered into existence: clench-fisted and on my back in the green of the Marchesa's chambers.

No more evening scent of time-bound night.

No more *profumi* of women and men beautiful in their finitude, their countenances lighting with the possibility of whatever their futures held. No fabrics fluted with gold. No future at all.

Screams upon my waking. Screams, and the acrid memory of smoke filling my head.

My eyes opened to the turquoise skyscape of the Marchesa's dressing room ceiling. I pushed myself up to a sitting position, jerking with sudden strength. I had gained years of youth, and my limbs shook uncontrollably. I screamed as my bones thickened and shortened in my skin. My limbs looked plumper, and as I ran my palms over my face, I felt smooth flesh free from hair.

The screams were distant; there was a commotion coming from the ballroom. As I hurried from the chamber and into the darkened corridor, I felt a crackling pain in my bones; with horror, I felt myself growing smaller, my limbs unsteadying.

I was growing younger, still.

The fire I had set in the Marchesa's timeline was not going out. It was killing more of his years, minutes, seconds as I ran – and I was being drained of years in tandem.

Cold terror filled my veins like a drug. I could not run from this. I only carried the one, spent vial of *acida notte*, and I could not travel back into the temporal realm to assist the Marchese's years in dousing the flames until I synthesized more.

"It is worth it," I heard myself growling. "If I am to die, it is worth it."

My clothes slid from me as I pressed on through the palazzo, heading to the light and sound of the ballroom below. I almost tripped over my cloak as it tangled about my legs. I was now the size of small child. Ten of the Marchese's years, at least, had been killed. And counting. I descended steps to the half-landing and peered between the marble bars, no longer tall enough to clear the balustrade.

The noblemen and women surged around the prostate form of the Marchese, Federico, convulsing in the middle of the rotunda. Men's and women's voices rose in confusion and terror. The Marchesa stood over her husband with an expression of madness and horror combined. There was no triumph in her face. I watched with keen eyes as Federico's skin folded into itself, the hair thinning and lightening as the years accelerated upon his body.

"Burn," I hissed, drunk with hate, hating him even more for making me feel hate at all. I had wanted to be happy in this life. "Burn for the gods. Burn." My pantaloons slipped down my waist and brushed my hips. I yanked at them, wriggling my arms through bagging sleeves.

The process was slowing. The Marchese was unconscious now, the body easing into old age. His clothes billowed around him as the form shrank, the muscles thinning to hew closer to his bones.

If the Marchese had been around forty years before I murdered his years, now... now he must have been near sixty. A decade and more gone in heartbeats.

And I... I was now a small child.

The crowd inched forward – and that was when the Marchesa looked up.

The impulse to live sparked in me, surprising as a lover's first kiss. I ran.

I heard her voice ringing out around the ballroom – "Catch the child! *Il ragazzino, il ragazzino* – catch him!" But the crowd surrounded her, servants rushing to attend the fallen Marchese di Lasciare, and I was down the stairs and through the throng of silks and sighs that were the men and women I could never touch, and never be. Ridiculous in robes made for a nobleman, crying tears in my wake, I ran out into the night.

The lights of the palace glared behind me, threatening at every moment to expose my unnatural form. I threw myself down alleyways, changing directions like a hare pursued. I headed for water.

My body was small now, a child's, and the clothes reared over me. I slipped out of them as if they had never belonged to me. Holding them to my chest and wrapping my jeweled cloak around me, I stumbled through the streets. A young urchin who made his home in the city's refuse traded me a set of children's garments, and some rations, for my own; his eyes glittered rapt in the dark starlight of the diamonds of my cloak. He could sell it all and eat for months, perhaps years. I withdrew a sheet of paper and a pen from its lining and, with shaking hands, scrawled a note. There was so much to say. So much I *could* say. Of the pain I had caused, the agony, all of it...

I wept. I wept for myself. I wept for the Marchese and Marchesa and all those others whose lives I had shortened. And here was I, a man of sixty years (or more) in the body of a boy, with the years before me. Or perhaps not. Perhaps there would be a respite; perhaps there would be a mercy. Perhaps she – the Marchesa – would give it to me. Hers was a keen mind, and she had proved herself a natural alchemist. She would find me and punish me for my wrongs, wretched as I was.

I listed the ingredients of the *acida notte* – cruel, horrid things, an insult to the gods! – and finished my note with these words:

Remember the anger you feel this night. Hold your hate for me close. It will give you strength, and the quenching of it, when you find me, will be exquisite. This work is hard but it helps us to survive the pain. It is for those broken hearts, the ones who have drunk deep from bitterness and seek a salve in the ruination of others: a stealing back of what has been stolen from us. I know I deserve to be punished – I know that – but knowing the secrets of acida notte, *you can now take your revenge on others in my stead. Redirect that anger. Keep it close. I am sorry. I am sorry for everything.*

I cursed the words; they could never convey the perverse glee at the thought that I was not alone in my suffering: that she, too, had been wounded now, and had been given the tools to undo that wounding. I gloried in her future revenge and at the same time hoped that it would never find *me*. The thought of punishment, of repentance, thrilled my heart – but death was unimaginable.

"Child, this cloak can be yours if you do one thing more for me. Can you deliver this note to the Palazzo di Lasciare without reading it?" I spoke to him through the tears. The boy nodded, barely able to look at me for the jewels. "Good." I folded the parchment and slipped it into his hand. "Hold it tight. Run straight to the palace, right now, and give it to the Marchesa."

I swung the cloak around his shoulders and he gasped in delight.

And then he was gone, and so was I, two runners streaking away into the night: one to the sea, and the other to the ruination I had left behind.

Years idled by. I lived them quietly, smuggling myself onto a ship headed for a distant shore, in a country not my own. I grew into my manhood yet again. The prickling of hairs on my body, the lengthening of my limbs drew fresh curses from my already cursed life. I was the pain and the parody of a man, perhaps seventy, perhaps eighty years old, looking no more than thirty. Perhaps a little older, perhaps younger... I had stopped being able to tell. It did not matter. None of it mattered, this time. No matter how many years I drained from others I grew into the same, hateful image: the same elongated face, the same grey eyes. The same lithe figure. How I was sick of it.

I took a lover, as I always took lovers, because I am weak and never learn. One man looked older than I, around fifty years old, and kind. We sailed on fragrant oceans and flew the night skies in *dirigibili*, eating the finest food and drinking the headiest wines. I, smiling and laughing and taking all of it, savoring all of it, because I knew that he too would leave me soon. I was sure of it.

I killed time less now, becoming more selective in my contracts, taking just enough to reverse the aging of my appearance when the first grey hairs streaked my temples and the skin around my eyes began to crease when I was happy. But it felt good, this starting over. And, after years of fear and doubt that most deadly of things – happiness – crept in.

I didn't want to believe she would find me; I had been distraught, reckless even, sending her the ingredients of the philter as I had done that night. Yet I had wounded her, made a murderess of her and scarred her with the guilt of what she, though unwitting, had brought about. Guilt did not rationalize, nor discriminate, though. I knew *that* too well. She would be scarred – and that scar, I hoped, would give her strength. Just not yet, not soon. The more years I enjoyed with my lover, the more I wanted. I was far from her. I heard nothing. I thought I had escaped. Stupidly, impossibly, I did the one thing I should not have done: I stopped running.

We were on a ship sailing the coast. It was summer, and the sun was bright, the wine cool and flowing. Youths played us music as nobles took their leisure and, yes, I was dressed in finery and felt, finally, that I belonged among them. I was happy.

My lover had gone to repose on the decks below, and I had kissed him and smiled before he left, promising to join him shortly. I would take in more of the sea air. Face-first to the sun, eyes closed – I smelled something rich: a new intoxication on the sea air. I turned and saw her standing behind me.

I did not recognize her at first. She looked older, a decade at least. She was dressed simply, her hair greying and unkempt.

Our eyes met.

Of course. Of course. This is only fair. I have had my cup of joy in this life; the rest is misery, and what I deserve.

She said nothing as she withdrew a vial from her breast. It was of clear green glass, and I did not have to ask what it contained. *Acida notte.*

I could have lunged forward, snatched it from her. But I was old. I was tired.

"You have come," I heard myself say. "Your *profumo* is exquisite."

"I know. I made it." She replied. Then, after heartbeats passed: "He died on the floor of the ballroom that night." Her face did not change its expression but I sensed the difficulty in her saying those words. "He didn't struggle. I don't know what you did but... you took too many years. It was too fast."

"It was an accident," I whispered.

"I did not ask for that. I am not to blame for that." She seemed not to have heard me. I saw that expression again: the turning-inward. The dialogue with herself. The conflict, and the reconciliation.

I said nothing. I waited for what was to come. I would give her everything she wanted: the perfect revenge. "Are you happy?" She asked me finally.

"I have known happiness."

"Good."

She pulled the cork from the potion.

"Not here," I said hurriedly. "You will fall into a stupor. Find yourself somewhere secure..."

But she was not listening. Stepping forward, her gown brushing against me, she leaned over the railing and drained the plague-green liquid into the ocean.

"I waited for a long time to find you," she said. "I hated you so much. So much hate that I did not even think possible... it was frightening. I imagined everything I would do. How much I would take from you. I hated you so fiercely – and you made me hate myself more for what I had brought about. But I forgave myself." She was weeping now, the sunlight making her tears golden streams on her cheeks. "And do you know something else?"

I shook my head. She looked into my face. The intimacy in her closeness was almost unbearable. "I forgave him, and... I forgive you too."

Something broke inside my chest. She saw it happen and said it again: "I forgive you."

"You can't!" I cried; I could not tolerate this, somehow this was worse, somehow –

"I forgive you." She said it again. "Gods! How many of us would be left alive if we were all to take revenge on the ones who hurt us? How many lifelines would be cut short? Do you think you are the only one whose heart hurts? Who has been wounded?" Her hands folded across her throat, alighting like birds.

"I do not deserve this... I do not..."

"I know. And yet you have it."

She did not hold me. I did not deserve that much mercy, and she would not disrespect herself. But she was there to witness the rocking of my body on that crystal sea, and the wind taking my cries, and the bucking and buckling of the inner structures that had kept my suffering contained: suffering that was everything and nothing at all. She was there to see the end of it. I opened my mouth to thank her again, and again –

"Enough." She raised a gloved hand. "It is done. Let us both live whatever futures we have left."

I looked at her, as if for the first time. The longer I looked the greater the mystery of her life became: a person more than her vengeance, more than her suffering. Where had she been born? How

did you spend her time? What meant most
to her in other people?

Other people.

I hadn't realized how beautiful and
complex people were before, for all that I
had roamed their temporal realms. The
clothes they put upon their bodies, how
they held themselves. How they sustained
their bodies – their *real* bodies – with food
and art and the million miracles of the
natural world. The sky. The earth
beneath. The winds that brought them
their breaths, the air moving within and
around them. Everything outside, here, *in
the physical world.* Where I was supposed
to be. Beholding everything real. *Acida
notte* opened a doorway that should never
have been opened. I beheld her and
realized that I had not been seeing the
world, truly, since the day I had been
wounded. *He* had turned me away from
the world. Now, at last, I wanted to return
to it.

She did not smile at me. She did
something more: she beheld me, in this
moment. As I was. More than I was. My
chest rose with gratitude that I could
never hope to voice, but wanted to voice
anyway...

She raised a hand, stopping me again. Not unkindly.

"No more, *ragazzino*. I have heard enough of your life. Go and live it."

See Phoenix Alexander's story "One for the Wounded" online at Metaphorosis.
If you liked it, leave a comment. Authors love that!
Remember to subscribe to our e-mail updates so you'll know when new stories are posted.

About the story

I was visiting family in Cyprus in the summer of 2018 and reading Alexander Chee's *The Queen of the Night* in the lazy, languid, 110-degree days. The sensory richness of the novel - the heightened emotion and drama of the narrative, the piled-on details of cloth and scent and stone - inspired me to try to write something similarly decadent.

At the same time, I had the notion to write about one of my greatest fears: the idea of wasting the time of one's life, of somnambulating through the days and years uncritically and leaving one's dreams and ambitions unfulfilled- and the realization of that waste that comes too late. This fear would be embodied by a protagonist who was kind of temporally stunted, and one who defined himself by his trauma. This aspect of the story was inspired by a particularly sad and troubled former room-mate of mine, who took all positivity and aid and comfort and sympathy and swallowed it like a black hole and, still, asked for more.

I wanted to process that as sympathetically as I could, and an important part of that process was dealing with the often impoverished models of love queer people 'inherit' or are normalized in. Finally, I wanted the Marchesa's character to represent the women whose time is wasted in the wake of gay men's affairs. Again, the challenge was to do all this with sympathy, and compassion, and something like hope: an anti-tragic-queer narrative. As difficult as it was for me to write, with "One for the Wounded" I aimed to turn the dross and banality of heartbreak into something beautiful.

A question for the author

Q: What work of art has been the most inspiring for you?

A: The work of art that has most inspired me over the years is Alfred Kubin's "The Symphony."

About the author

Phoenix Alexander is a queer, Greek-Cypriot scholar and writer of science fiction. Born in Cyprus, he was raised in England and has been moving steadily westward ever since. Initially training as fashion designer in London, he swiftly realized the error of his ways and has just completed a PhD in English and African American Studies at Yale University.

www.phoenixalexanderauthor.com, @dracopoullos

In the Beating of a Wing

David Cleden

When his mother calls, Chester is in the back yard tending to his various projects, which all seem to be going badly.

"Chester!" Her voice is shrill and tired-sounding, as though she's been crying again. "Inside now, please."

He ignores her, head bent over his work.

The frankenstem is dying, and he's sad about that.

The books he's read make it sound easy—how you can graft cuttings from one plant onto another, taking the best parts from two different things and combining them. Simple, really. So, with a stolen kitchen knife, Chester has made little diagonal incisions into the bark of the young willow growing in a shady corner of the yard. He's spliced a variety of scavenged off-shoots into those cuts to make his 'frankenstem.' There's the head of a pink rose (already long past its best and beginning to wilt, so he's not hopeful it will survive this drastic transplant), the sticky tip of a sweet chestnut flower, the root-stock of a petunia dug up from his mother's window-box and—his personal favorite—a bramble thorn with a wickedly sharp point. Threads of cotton teased from his fraying t-shirt bind each of the grafted items in place. The result isn't pretty, but that was never the point. He wants to see what survives and what doesn't.

Only... It's been a few hours now, and the frankenstem grafts look pale and limp, browning at their cut edges. Even the willow has begun oozing sticky sap from its wounds.

"Chester!" Louder this time, her patience ebbing.

The yard is a safe-haven, more so than the house. Although the house is familiar (and that's good, of course) it often has people in it. The kind of people it attracts are mostly his mother's friends—exactly the kind Chester dislikes. All they seem to want to do is talk. Some of them even want to talk to *him*.

Not that he replies. His mother despairs of him because he won't talk to her. To anyone, in fact.

It's been two hundred sixty one days since Chester last spoke aloud. Mostly, he has nothing that needs saying. And now it's become one of his experiments. He's curious: how long is it possible to go without talking? Can he live his whole life this way? He doesn't think he will, but it's an interesting experiment all the same.

Of course, some of his experiments turn out better than others. His taste experiment, for example, when he sampled every type of living plant he could find growing in the yard, carefully recording the outcome. The results were interesting, but he was sick for three days after.

"Chester! Are you ignoring me?"

A tiny moth brushes against his face, tickling his skin. It alights on the frankenstem and starts climbing upwards, stopping every few steps as though inspecting Chester's work. Its wings beat a frantic rhythm, the sound of paper fluttering in the breeze.

There are dozens of them in the yard. His mother's friends complain about them all the time. What if they turn out to be dangerous? Suppose the mutation spreads? Something ought to be done.

Chester leans closer, peering at the tiny vibrating body. Is it dangerous? It doesn't look dangerous. It's just a moth, barely the size of his thumbnail. A bullet-shaped body, vaguely triangular wings. He's read up its Latin name: *lymantria dispar*, the gypsy moth. In pictures, they look a speckled brown, but this one is a crisp white, as though the creature has been fashioned out of icing sugar. A mutation has occurred in the species, fundamentally changing it right down in its DNA, the scientists are saying. 'Engineered' is a word that gets used a lot. But it's a mystery who the engineers might be, or their purpose.

He's listened to the wilder theories discussed on the late-night TV channels when he's supposed to be asleep: clandestine government laboratories with their gene-editing programs, or secretive terrorist cells creating some kind of bio-weapon, or alien spores drifting across the cosmos.

Chester likes to lie in his bed at night, imagining a world so far away, its sun is not even a faint prick of light in our night sky. The beings who inhabit this system carefully select some desolate, icy world, impregnate it with their engineered virus until it takes hold in every crack and pore, like a farmer sowing a crop. Then they explode that world into a billion pieces; an expanding sphere of debris, each a messenger to the waiting stars. A long time passes—but the originators understand what it means to be patient. Sooner or later, these long-dormant icy fragments will be woken from a millennia-long slumber.

He imagines one such fragment nudged by the chance perturbations of celestial mechanics. Finally tickled by the Sun's warmth, it sloughs off an outer skin of complex organic molecules. When the Earth strays into the tenuous trail left behind, the alien material mingles with wisps of atmosphere and tropospheric winds carry it around the globe. Instructions are followed: simple replicating patterns infiltrate whatever primitive living structures they encounter and slowly—

Chester's arm is yanked backwards and he almost falls.

"How dare you ignore me, young man! Haven't I warned you about being out here when those horrible moths are around? Get back in the house this instant!"

His mother pulls him back across the yard, his feet dragging. He turns to look back at his frankenstem one last time, but the moths have moved on.

Jeanette Briggs feels the tension mounting inside her: a prickling sensation crawling across her forehead, cramp in her hand as she clutches the phone in a death grip. "I just want my son to be *normal,* Dr Pattaya," she says, fighting to keep her voice even, and not quite succeeding.

"The fact is, Mrs. Briggs, Chester won't ever be that, not in the sense you mean. Remember we talked about the autism spectrum?"

"More *engaged,* then. Why won't he talk to me anymore? To anyone?"

There's a gentle sigh from the other end of the line. Jeanette imagines the consultant psychologist rocking back in a deep-padded chair, probably gazing up at ceiling vents from which deliciously chilled air cascades into the room. She herself is sweating like a pig in this early summer heat. Damp spots stick the cotton dress to her skin. Dark motes dance in her vision every time she moves her head.

"We've established that Chester is perfectly engaged," Dr Pattaya is saying. "But on his own terms. There is no physical impairment of speech. When he wants to, he'll speak again."

Jeanette stares out the kitchen window to the back yard. Even more of the horrible flittery moth-things are in evidence, settling on the shrubs like hoar-frost, or fluttering in ever-changing clouds amongst the tree branches. She hates them. Some damn scientist has been playing god again—or, saints preserve us, some terrorist group.

None of the TV talking-heads seem to think the moth mutations are a threat. At least, not yet. The mutation hasn't been seen in neighboring species, and its detrimental effects seem to be limited to some minor behavioral changes. Infected moths exhibit an odd gregariousness; an unnatural tendency to swarm in a way never observed before. And of course, there's the extreme albino trait, that pristine snowy-whiteness.

Nothing to worry about, mutters the TV in the corner. *Everything necessary is being done.*

It's just that there are so many of them, Jeanette thinks. More every day. And if some kind of viral infection is behind it all, no one can say where it might have come from.

Right now, two or three are batting ineffectually against the window pane. She looks past their milky, pearlescent bodies to where Chester stands in the yard. With a jolt of panic, she sees he's as still as a statue, a cloud of white moths surrounding him like a halo. Ugh. Arms outstretched, he's trying to get them to alight on him. But they dance and flutter just out of range.

She raps on the glass, gesturing him to come inside. It's not as if she doesn't have enough things to worry about.

Chester hears. He glances back towards the house, then he turns his back on her.

Oh, that boy! Now she'll have to go out there and fetch him again.

On the phone, Dr Pattaya is droning on in the same professional monotone, the one carefully cultured to impart either good or bad news with equanimity. But something he's just said—

"Wait," she says. "Tell me that part again. I'm interested in any new treatments you've got, no matter how experimental."

It turns into a much longer phone call and Jeanette bites her lip with indecision as she listens, all the time watching Chester through the window.

The TV whispers to itself in the corner. Jeanette catches enough to get the drift while she cooks dinner. Never anything new to report, of course, only endlessly recycled speculation.

"—virus mutation unlike anything seen before, but impossible to say where—"

"—DNA-like structures, but also a previously unknown nucleobase which has been dubbed—"

"—emergence of a completely new type of virus. But why? We just don't know."

Why?

Everything circles back to that one question that no one has an answer to.

Mom talks and talks, trying to make him understand.

He understands perfectly. But he can't let her know, not even with a shake or a nod of the head, because that would be like saying yes or no—and then the experiment would be ruined. Two hundred sixty seven days of silence. He's come too far to abandon it now, not until there's something worth saying.

"I promise it won't hurt, Chester. The electrodes that go inside your head are tiny. They're going to tickle your brain. See if they can wake up some parts that are sleeping right now. I know that sounds scary, but Dr Pattaya has promised it won't hurt. And when it's all over, you'll feel so much better! You'll feel..."

She stops before she can tell him how it will make him feel. Normal? Is that what she means? It's a word she's often used when talking with Dr Pattaya.

Does he want to feel normal? Not if it means he can't do his experiments any more. Not if it means he has to stop being himself.

"So the day after tomorrow, we're going to see Dr Pattaya in the hospital. Just for a few days. He'll take good care of you and I'll be with you the whole time. Is that okay with you, Chester?"

No. It isn't okay.

This is the closest he's come to abandoning the experiment. It's a real struggle. He wants to shake his head or scream out, "No!"

But he's put so much into this. He can't ruin the experiment now. Besides, Mom never used to listen to him before. Why would it be any different now?

His mother bats away a moth that lands on his bedside lamp-shade. "Ugh! Horrible things!"

She'd be horrified if she knew that earlier, he opened his window wide, hoping a few of the transformed *lymantria dispar* would be drawn by the warm bedroom light. They fascinate him. Through a magnifying glass, their bullet-shaped bodies remain curiously fuzzy, like someone's rough pencil sketch. They always seem to be in motion; their wings beating in a blur even when settled. There's much more he must find out about them...

Mom knocks the moth to the floor and steps on it. Its body crunches and becomes a smear of whitish powder on the rug.

"Horrible things," she repeats.

Chester looks at her, his expression unreadable.

But he says nothing.

Later that night Chester hears the drones flying. Mom has closed all the windows, blocked up the fireplace—house sealed tight in the way the authorities have instructed. But she can't stop him watching from the window as the fine mist of chemicals falls like gentle rain. Again and again, the drones fly complicated patterns above the city, breaking off now and then to refill at distant tanker stations before flying to the next sector.

By morning, their yard is white with moth carcasses, like a weird kind of snowfall. It's impossible to step outside without treading on them. All dead; millions upon millions of them. Their bodies crunch underfoot and turn to a fine dust.

"Tomorrow," Mom tells him, "is a really important day. A day you'll look back on and be glad of."

A lie. But he's getting better at recognizing them.

He wonders if he should run away, just for a while. It wouldn't be hard to stuff some food and clothes into a backpack and sneak out of the house. Where would he go, though? It's such a scary thing to think about. And the idea of going outside revolts him. It means trampling on a carpet of dead moths and he couldn't bear that.

So he stays in his room, door shut, refusing to come out all day. Mom doesn't get angry. She brings his meals on a tray, smiling in that fake way of hers he's come to associate with her feeling guilty.

He doesn't want to go to the hospital. He remembers Dr Pattaya: an overweight man with an unwavering gaze, smelling of stale sweat. He gave every appearance of listening intently to what Chester said— back before Chester began his experiment in silence—but moments later it was all dismissed as an irrelevance.

Nobody listens. Nobody ever sees things as they really are.

And now everything's turning out wrong.

Swarms of *lymantria* have been wiped out in their millions. The frankenstem experiment has failed. Through the window, he can see the willow drooping and forlorn in the corner of the yard. It was a stupid idea. You can't build something new just by bolting bits and pieces together. You have to strip things down to their basic components and build afresh.

Should he abandon his other experiments, too?

He listens, making sure Mom isn't hovering outside his room like she sometimes does. Carefully, he opens the wardrobe door, removing a small off-cut of willow. A tiny white moth clings to it, wings trembling. It may be the very last of the altered *lymantria*. He offers it a morsel of food from his plate, but the creature seems frozen and moribund, as though mourning the loss of its siblings. By suppertime, its wings no longer beat. Gently, Chester strokes its tiny, delicate back. At his touch, the moth crumples into dust.

He feels something then. There are things he dimly recognizes as descriptions of sorrow, hurt, and anger, all churning inside him like the drum of the kitchen washer. Even so, the emotions are cold and clinical, serving no purpose that he can see. He had expected more.

Only his curiosity is undiminished.

He stares at the remains of the *lymantria*. On a whim, and remembering his ill-fated garden taste experiment, he licks a finger, dips it into the gray residue and puts it to his tongue. Does anyone know what space-moths taste of?

He senses a grittiness between his teeth as though something has been ground down into its constituent parts. But as for taste, all he can savor is the saltiness of his own skin.

There is a hard rain that night. Not the quiet mist of drone-sprayed insecticide, but a driving downpour pounding against the shingles and running in rivulets to the gutters. It washes away the white-dust remains of the moths, scouring the roads and sidewalks of their crushed bodies. Almost as if they had never existed.

Chester is not sleeping. Strange, flickery thoughts slide through his mind, like watching some bad stop-motion film; all jerky and indistinct.

He's running a fever. Feeling sick. He stumbles out of bed to let some cool night air into the room. The rain has stopped but the air is laden with its moisture, and there's a tang of something else, too.

Before long, a dark shape flutters through the open window, alighting on the bed. Soon, two more join it. Their wingbeats are just a blur. If he blinks rapidly, he can see flickering patterns of iridescence in their wings, like the spokes of a wheel in some old western that seem to turn the wrong way.

More moths are arriving, streaming into the room. They aren't the altered *lymantria*. These are crudely-shaped creatures; gray-black blobs with small, fast-beating wings, like some child's model built out of left-over parts of other insects. Frankenmoths? They swarm and pulse in odd shapes at the end of the bed, as more crowd in through the open window to join the swarm.

Their wings make tiny, meaningless patterns. He blinks, trying to make sense of it, but the patterns dance and change too fast.

Thoughts that are not his own run free in his mind—

Ready?

"Yes," he says, and the voice he hears is barely more than a croak. His own voice; a strange and unfamiliar sound. It's been such a long time. Two hundred sixty eight days precisely. But now there's something important that needs saying.

Jeanette calls up the stairs. "Get in the car please, Chester. It's time."

She knows he won't, that she'll have to go up to his room and maybe drag him out. He spends far too much time up there now, staring into space as if listening to things that only he can hear. If this treatment doesn't work, what on earth is she going to do?

Jeanette does a last scan round the kitchen. Purse, car keys, overnight bag for Chester. She can't put the moment off any longer. "Chester!" she yells one final time. When she turns to climb the stairs, she nearly jumps out of her skin because Chester is on the bottom step. He's standing very still. His face is composed but she gets a sense of something pent up inside, something about to break free.

"Come and see," he says.

Her brain takes a few moments to register what's just happened.

He spoke to you.

He spoke!

Chester disappears back upstairs.

"Wait—"

She follows him into the bedroom, her hands flying to her mouth, stifling a scream. Moths are still streaming in through the open window, like ghostly wisps of dark smoke twisting and turning in a non-existent breeze. They spool themselves onto the mass of bodies circulating above the bed, becoming a dense cluster of black, vibrating blobs packing together so tightly the sound of tiny wings brushing against each other becomes a roar of static, like a receiver not yet tuned to a station.

"What's happening?"

There's a snowstorm of beating wings against the glass. They rise up out of the storm-drains. They crawl from puddles, clamber glistening and new-born from streams and rivers. Transformation is swift. Instructions which have lain dormant in the alien virus for millennia are re-activated. New forms arise from the organic building blocks of the decomposing *lymantria*.

There's so much that needs saying now. Chester can feel the subtle changes taking place deep inside. He's ready. The virus has found its target host at last, like a lock that fits its key. An image floats into his mind: strands of DNA-like material unwinding like threads being pulled from an old sweater—or the cotton threads binding those crude grafts on his frankenstem. Now the DNA reforms in a new arrangement, patiently replicating its message carried from a distant world across eons of time.

"It's calibrating," he tells her. "The message is decoding." He takes a step towards the tight ball of insect bodies.

"Chester, don't—"

She seizes his shoulders. "You're scaring me. What message? Who's sent it?"

Chester stretches out a hand and one of the dusky black bodies settles on a fingertip. Its tiny wings are so delicate they shimmer with iridescence, flitting through rainbow colors like a visual test pattern. When he offers it to her for inspection, she shrinks back. "I don't understand."

The ball is coalescing, holding position in the air above Chester's bed, a dense mass of fluttering bodies.

"They must have waited a long time to talk to us, Mom."

"Who's they, Chester?"

He shrugs. "Let's find out."

The wings begin to beat in time, a throbbing sphere built from the roiling mass of insect bodies. Subtle changes in wingbeat frequency sweep ripples of multi-colored moiré patterns across the surface. They slow and settle into pulsing waves. Each beating wing becomes a single pixel in a vast, three-dimensional array.

Chester laughs and claps his hands.

Moving images begin to form.

The message begins.

See David Cleden's story "In the Beating of a Wing" online at Metaphorosis.
If you liked it, leave a comment. Authors love that!
Remember to subscribe to our e-mail updates so you'll know when new stories are posted.

About the story

I work from home a lot and one day I looked up from my computer to see a pretty little moth on the outside of the window. I watched it for a while, assuming it would soon fly away, but it didn't. It walked across the glass to the corner of the window nearest my desk and stayed there for half an hour or more. What fascinated me was the way its wings kept beating the whole time. It wasn't caught in a web and stayed in contact with the glass the whole time, so as far as I could see there was no reason for its wings to keep beating. The longer I watched, the more I felt as if the moth knew I was there and was trying to communicate with me, fluttering its tiny wings in ever-changing rhythms.

It seemed an idea too good to pass up, and I started scribbling story notes right away. Before I could finish, the moth must have decided its work was done, the message sent, and it fluttered off. But we had shared our special moment, and that was enough.

A question for the author

Q: What book or books inspired you as a child?

A: At some point in my childhood reading, I came across the science fiction of Isaac Asimov. I loved those novels about time travellers and robot detectives and far-future galactic empires. Then in the local library one day, I came across an anthology of science fiction stories, each of which had a little personal introduction by Asimov and suddenly it was as if he was not only telling me wonderful stories but speaking directly to me. I'd never met any writers at that point. There were no websites or internet. But here was Isaac Asimov reaching out to his readers and chatting with them about anything and everything as though we were firm friends. More than anything, that proximity to someone that I admired so much convinced me that one day I wanted to be a science fiction writer too.

Later I discovered Asimov's books of science essays gathered from his monthly column in "Fantasy and Science Fiction" magazine. They, too, began with some personal note or chatty introduction. His writing style made every difficult concept seem accessible. Suddenly I was convinced I wanted to study science and be a science fiction writer, something I still aspire to today.

About the author

David Cleden is a British author. He hasn't led a colourful life, doesn't live in an exotic location and possesses little in the way of interesting hobbies, so he tries to make up for all this by writing speculative fiction.

www.quantum-scribe.com, @davidcleden

The Memory Dresser

Nicholas M. Stillman

Our parlor is small—tucked in a corner of Helm, folded between an empty Gassa stall and the home of a half-deaf mystic. For this reason, discretion numbers as one of our services. Not even the moon bears full witness, as Illsea, the largest Tower on the hill, shades us from the first few hours of evening light. Under our lamps, we shape the memories of the people of Helm, our people. Unlike the royals in Illsea, they are not looking for beauty. No shine-oil treatments or the newest configuration of knots and trellises. Our client's memories are coated in the dirt that lines our streets and our teeth. They sit in my grandmother's chair and weep at their reflections. Each length tracks the harrowing years of their lives in the dim lamps or beady sun: yesterday's shame growing from their scalp, their unfortunate births dragged through the streets. My grandmother's job is to make them feel well—to clean and wrap, braid and twist them into people who can walk back into their lives without shame dragging them down.

My own memories are unremarkable. Ordinary, frizzed, limp. My childhood must have been something to forget, because I all but have. There are a few years, though, that are different. Four finger lengths that hold the light like river rocks after rain. Memories that burst forth like the sweet juices of thin-fleshed berries, eclipsing all other flavor. My mother excited, touching my shoulder, pointing at the marigolds and the poppies not yet in bloom around the village pond. Fresh bread and cool paya juice as the fireworks erupt above the Towers during the New Sun dance. Then, below the shore rocks we clambered onto, the rich Oversea folk filing in and out of their boats—their strange memories gleaming in impenetrable designs, fractals upon fractals. Mother's breath curling warmly in the cold night onto my scalp and tips of my ears, running her thin fingers through my memories while we watched the beautiful people glisten. *One day*, her voice sounds as if she were still beside me, *you'll have memories like that.*

Whenever I felt the dull ache of boredom begin to blossom throughout my body, I would twine these strands between my fingers, feeling their health against my skin, or else tie the lengths around my forehead so that everyone who met me met the finest version.

"If your chin were any higher you'd break your neck," said Grandmother, tugging at the steeple knot holding my best memories in view. "You want the world to think you're better than them? Who are you to do that?" She would make me fold them beneath less pleasant memories. Dull evenings in the parlor. Sweaty days jostling through the market's center. Father's long trips dragging a net into salty water for exotic hues of sea life to be shipped and filleted and served to the people he despised most. My mother's last year, bed-bound and shivering.

Grandmother was disdainful of the extravagant. She despised my secret yearnings for things I had seen: marigolds and poppies and beautiful memories rippling like the sea as the Oversea folk slipped onto boats. She preferred a meek life of quiet dignity, a healthy distrust of laughter.

One morning, before the clients lined out her door, she cut a sheet into strips with my father's old gutting knife and, leaving one end intact and tied to the Dressing chair, she pressed the strips into my sweating palms. Grandmother turned the strands one by one—revealing the sheet's bloodstain, oil spot, jagged edges, holes from ash. I nodded. I folded strips into one another, braided them, looped them, curled them with brass rollers. My fingers were small but eager as I worked a loose approximation of the Sargusoa style —limp and casual, with two elaborate loops. I made sure to hide each imperfection beneath the cleaner lengths. My memory Dressing would impress upon others the wearer's connection to a rich childhood, as the brightest ends of sheet I bent at angles that would catch the sunlight. When I finished, I dabbed sweat from my forehead and smiled.

Grandmother slapped my cheek.

"Look what you've done." She flipped over my knots, pointed to the blood, oil, jagged edges I'd disguised.

"It looks better this way," I said, my voice faltering.

"So like your mother." She said it as a curse. She pulled at my release thread and the Sargosa collapsed back into a tattered sheet. When she saw my eyes filling with anger, my fists balling, she cocked her head. "What, you want a village of pretenders? Whoever hides the best is the winner? You want your people to think they have to compete with each other, compete with the Towers? All they do is try to survive. Don't take that from them."

I bit back tears. I could not imagine letting a client walk out with their poverty, their abuses and vices and regrets plain in the sun for all to see. Surely there was a way to cover them? "Why should there always be something to hide? Not everyone is so miserable."

"There will always be stains," she said, cutting down the sheet and twisting the strands to be dipped in oil and used as lantern wicks. "These people are decent, Helm people. They don't want to be glamorized like an oiled Tower empress.

They want to be understood. That is why we do not hide pasts, but weave the hurt and joy together so that both catch the light. Our job is to frame their lives in such a way that others can see dignity, not glamor, not suffering. We cannot afford to play games with our memories Not here." I followed her eyes to the dust whistling through the empty street, the sun already baking the walking boards stretched between the gutters. Illsea loomed over us, its shadow not yet cast.

Days in the parlor turned like the trapped figurine of a music box while my memories grew stale. The same clients to seat, well buckets to drag, lavender to pick, stones to heat, cloth to wash, rice to cook. I waited. I cut my sheets into strips. Practiced in the moonlight before the tower eclipsed the light. I snuck pamphlets of the latest Dressing styles from the market and slid them under my mattress. I exercised my fingers and wrists. I trained myself for a life I was better suited to.

Then, one night, after I had closed the doors and drawn the sunshade over the window, a confident knock rapped at the door. Then another.

"Oh, go on," Grandmother sighed, no doubt preparing her speech—*Your memories will still be there in the morning.*

At the door, however, was not Ginja the mystic who wanted to sell us another memory-reading, but a stranger. She was tall and lean, her neck long and seamless. A dark cloak was draped over her shoulders and a dust wrap pleated neatly over her face so that her dark eyes and long lashes poked through like hermit crab antenna. She stepped through me as if I occupied no space at all.

Before Grandmother could speak, the woman flipped the cloak off of her shoulders, revealing a white silk tunic and her loose-wrapped memories shining like polished ore in the lamplight. A medallion of Illsea hung from her neck. I lost the ability to move.

She glided to the dressing chair in silence and seated herself. A chair that had, only minutes before, held Malik, who bathed once a week in the camel water trough. She crossed her legs and examined the shelves cluttered with abandoned dressing equipment—rusted iron clips and outdated bows. My cheeks burned.

Grandmother wiped her hands on her tunic. Wiped them again. She did not speak. Only stood like a low-cast shadow, clearing her throat to no avail.

The woman spoke without turning her head. "Girl, what's your name?"

Grandmother opened her mouth to respond, but realized too late that she was not the girl.

"Mina," I managed in a hoarse whisper.

"Do you live here?"

"My room is upstairs."

"Mina, this is my daughter, Tengi."

I turned, startled to find a small, dark girl standing just inside the door. She seemed to be everything her mother was not—short, wide-hipped with small eyes and a flat face. She was pretty in her own way, and prettier still than anyone I'd seen in the parlor besides her mother.

"Please take Tengi up to your room to play while I speak with the Dresser."

Tengi made a face that indicated she would rather run with street dogs than climb the thin wooden staircase to my room. I searched Grandmother's eyes for guidance, but found none. Her body was rigid, as if a wild animal had entered the room.

Tengi was already marching petulantly to the staircase. I followed. Her memories bounced before my eyes as we climbed. Her head was covered in a silken maroon cloth and a thick braid fell down and wrapped around her waist. The braid was deeper and richer than the silk covering, making the latter look cheap; the kind of cloth we would sell unfaithful spouses attempting to disguise their guilt. I marveled. It was as if Tengi's entire life had been fireworks and fresh bread. With a start I realized Grandmother was wrong —not everyone had stains.

That first evening, and several after, Tengi refused to speak to me. We would sit in silence, Tengi's hands clasped in her lap, face turned up to Illsea, as we waited for my grandmother to finish her secret work. Later, Tengi brought a book and read it when there was enough light. Finally, one night when Tengi's eyes were wild with anger, her memory scattered about her shoulders, she spoke:

"You should apply a Barosa nut oil twice a day if you don't want your memories to collect all that dust."

I nodded. I felt that a critical gap had been bridged. I let loose all of my caged questions. About her purpose in my room, her mother in our shop, her bedroom in the Tower, her thick, syrupy memories. But my questions were like throwing stones at a circling hawk. Tengi watched them with interest before diving: *Tell me, what's it like being so poor?*

Our words began to search out our differences, curiously prodding each other's edges. Each revelation was like a flash river after a rain as we encouraged more questions. I surprised her with my knowledge of the latest Dressing styles, my love of the Oveasea fractal knots, my awareness of the various uses of poppies and marigolds. And she both surprised me and didn't surprise me; every detail a revelation I could not have anticipated. The Tower competitions for memory shine, the strong-necked men tying their memories together and pulling like reluctant lovers until one buckled, the heartbreak of the smallest memory imperfections, the scandal of memory painting. "There are some who refuse to do anything but fuck and eat and travel before a dance," she'd said, her language embarrassing me. "There are servants who shield them from crumbs. Some refuse to see their children in case the child cries or falls or misspeaks, and so taints their memories. The competition is shit. And yet if you don't do those things, you stand alone at the dance and your memories get even weaker. There's no way out."

"And here you will be ridiculed for trying too hard," I said, breathless. "If I try to clean Malik's tangle or hide his embarrassment with a clip or cloth, Grandmother would call me a pretender. Nothing I do is allowed to be beautiful."

Tengi and I spent our nights comparing our lives while the two women worked and the constellations did slow battle through the slats of my roof. Sometimes we would climb out my window and wander to the spice fields and rub Tougo into our teeth, sometimes we would chance a trip to the market when the sun was still up and hold hands and call each other *beloved* to watch the old men bend incline their heads at our parting. I knew that every week Tengi would arrive at my doorstep, and she did without fail. I had never met anyone like her and she, she confided one night, had never met anyone like me. Her presence textured my days and gave a shape to my daily life.

As the weeks wore on, there were more Dressings, which meant more Tengi in my life. Tengi did not tell me why her mother came so much often than other clients, but I knew the New Sun dance was approaching and I guessed there was some secret vanity, or problem that needed mending before the start. When I did glimpse her mother, mostly from my window as I watched Tengi leave, I saw that she looked vacant, her steps unnecessarily cautious. Tengi would guide her by the hand away from the shop to wherever the escorts had hidden the carriage.

One night, while the moths threw their bodies at my window, we touched memories. It was late—the women below us were working long, as usual. It was Tengi's idea. To have me practice working with healthy memory, to prepare for the day she would bring me to the Towers as her personal Dresser. I asked her to show me what they did in Illsea, how the Dressers prepared. She swallowed as she loosened her tunic and dropped it down below her bare shoulders, shook her memories out of its braid. I listened to the tapping of moths trying to hurl themselves at my lamp.

We sat on our knees, facing each other, the flesh of our thighs touching.

Tengi's memories were like ripples in water. So bright they felt like liquid glass, or something else I could not describe. My breath came in small gasps as her fingers danced along the hollow strands of my boredom and routine, clicking her tongue lightly. My eyes fluttered and the floor groaned as we delved deeper into each other's lives. I felt something shift beneath my breastbone. A stirring.

I worked my fingers up her memory, then allowed my fingers to explore the hidden days and weeks beneath the maroon silk covering. Tengi screamed. Scrambled away from me, gathering spare bits of herself and pinning them behind her. I didn't know what I'd done wrong.

Tengi reluctantly untied the maroon cloth, and I saw it. Falling just above the tip of her ear, was a section of memory that was white and hollow as a feather's heart. The kind of loss I thought only those in Helm had experienced. I tracked the growth with practiced eyes. She had been carrying it silently since the week we'd met.

"Tengi, I—what happened?"

She smoothed the memory behind her, clipping them back. "I forgot. I'm sorry. I should have warned you."

I stood, angry and frightened and still drunk off her touch. "What happened? Who did this?"

She shook her head.

"Why is your mother here? Why are you here? Please. You need to tell me."

Tengi opened her mouth, closed it. She stood and went to the window, to look up at the Tower. Her Tower. "These memories are the same ones my mother has. The ones my mother is paying your grandmother to cut."

"What?"

Tengi slid open the window and the moths went in search of their flame. "They would kill her if anyone knew."

"I—cut?" The thought churned in my stomach; a mutilation I had not considered. To cut memories was a heinous act, punishable by execution. Killing a person ended their life, but cutting them ended who they were. Who would choose to lose themselves?

"She wants to forget." Tengi turned to look at me, her mouth clenched in a smile. "And now I am the only one who will remember." She passed her face through the window, closed her eyes.

I didn't know what to do, what to say. I had so many questions, knew so little. Silent, I walked behind her, closed my eyes, and joined her, our faces waiting for a breeze.

My grandmother and I took to standing like hungry cats by the door on the days we knew they would come. We turned away clients, as neither of us could focus until they arrived. They were our great secrets. Grandmother spoke less about my attraction to dreaminess, my selfishness, even as I lingered in front of the Dressing mirror turning my head to admire how my new memories seemed to brighten my eyes, add color to my cheeks. In my reflection I saw an open, bright person. Someone brimming with possibility.

Tengi snuck me Tower oil and ribbons and when Grandmother was not around I would walk into the market with my most

recent memories oiled. I shimmered in the
heat. In return, I said nothing to
Grandmother about the cutting. She
would stop her work if she thought I
knew, and I could not risk losing Tengi.

Tengi was changing, too. Her memories
were growing crooked. She took to hiding
them with bows and expensive ribbon.
She shrank from touch if I approached
her too quickly, moved too quietly. Wind
from the streets would cause her to spasm
in fear and it would take me minutes of
careful teasing to distract her. I never
touched her recent growth and it pained
me that we had becomes so different. I
would try to find gaps in conversation to
ask her about the white growth, what had
happened to her, and how I could help. All
I wanted to do was help. Tengi told me not
to worry, nothing was my fault, it wasn't
me.

One evening, after Tengi and her mother
had gone, father arrived. He greeted us
without his right foot—a result of a
rationing mistake on board his ship and
several short straws drawn in a life of
short straws. It had been years since he'd

been home, and I barely recognized the man from my childhood. His memory was thick and clotted and smelled of fish viscera and left an oily trail like a slug.

After an awkward and stilted embrace, he sniffed my memories, and I became aware of the thick, nutty oil still seated there. His eyes wandered to Grandmother, who hid behind her the old gutting knife she used for cutting. At her feet lay the strands of two dead memories she had yet to sweep from the floor.

I felt his hand tighten around my shoulder. "This is what happens when I leave?" he spat. "I ought to turn you in for risking my wife's parlor. *My* rightful parlor."

"It's not like that," I said, unable to release myself from his grip. "They came from Illsea, they're not like you think."

He rounded on me. For a moment, while he had me pinched in his grip, I thought he would flay me like a fish, his muscles having formed the habit.

Seeing the terror in my eyes seemed to shift something in him.

He released me. Searched me for what felt like signs of someone else. Someone who was not me.

"I'm home now. For good," he said as if reminding himself. "Illsea took my foot and then dropped me on the shore. So if either of you think you still want to play your Tower games, then maybe I'll have to cut those memories from you myself." His face crinkled in pain, his eyes darted to the memories of my childhood. "Your mother would never have wanted this. Never this."

In the months that followed, I would often lie in bed, tracking the sun's progress across my floor. Grandmother stopped promising to train me, and I stopped collecting pamphlets from market, stopped practicing on my sheets. I watched my father's memories grow out white. Grandmother tried to clean them, to dress them lightly, but he refused her, preferring to wallow.

The few decent memories I had made with Tengi began to fade as dull, frizzed ones pushed them down my neck. I could no longer face the market, watch their eyes take in how far I had fallen. I became angry with Tengi for her ability to continue on with her life while I sat in the same room she'd found me in, waiting for her to return. I felt our lives together slipping further into my past and wondered if she felt that distance, too. If she even noticed.

The rains came. I grew hollow, forgetful. Grandmother covered my memories with a dashini so that I would have enough courage to leave the room. I refused to remove it, even at my grandmother's pleading for memories to have light and air. In her mind, a little damage was better than hiding completely. But I knew she was wrong. The more you show the damage, the more of you it becomes, until it is all you are.

And then, on the eve of the New Sun dance, Tengi climbed through my window. She smelled of the red dirt from the back roads below the Towers. She must have ridden all day.

"Tengi?" I stood perfectly still, just as I had the day her mother first entered our parlor. "What…Why are you here?"

Tengi's face was stretched tight, her memories frizzed and loose, dragging behind her. She pulled it through the window.

"Because I need help," she said.

"Where have you been?" I felt my surprise leaking into bitterness. "Why didn't you come back for me?"

Tengi shrugged past me. She cradled something heavy in her coat. "I am watched, my mother and me. When your grandmother sent word that she would no longer..." she lifted her head, thinking. "The message was discovered. Now I can't piss without someone holding my hand."

I did not know what to say, how to respond, what to do with the anger I had been holding for her—anger for abandoning me here, stranding me in a desert with my father.

"What do you want?"

Tengi placed a silken maroon bundle from her coat onto my bed. I recognized the cloth as the one that once covered her damage. "I want you to help me," she said, staring at the cloth. "I am not going to the dance. There is not a skilled enough Dresser in the world to hide all of this." She found my eyes with hers.

"You came to tell me that?"

"I am going on a boat. Oversea."

I approached her as if she might, at any moment, collapse into nothing. I was still unsure of her, but my mind filled with new possibilities. Boats. Dances. I absently recalled those years with my mother, as I often did, the memories still burning brightly in my mind. "And how do you want me to help you?" I said coolly.

Tengi looked at me with what might have been hurt at my tone. Or sadness. "Oh," she said. "I want you to come with me."

My mouth dried. The room shifted slightly. "But I thought you wanted my help."

"That's part of it. I... I'm leaving whether or not you come. But I want you too."

"Oh." I could not think of what to say. I touched my dashini, recalling how much I'd changed. I felt weak at my inability to move on without her. I resented her for it.

"I need to show you something," Tengi said as she kneeled and unwrapped the bundle. Beneath the maroon silk lay a dagger. A thin blade wide as my finger and long as my hand, with a handle of pearl. I stepped back, knocking a book from my shelf. It thudded to the floor, and I heard my father shifting in his bed beneath us. He rarely slept, and his temper was deep and treacherous in the middle of the night. I held my breath.

"I need you," Tengi said, picking the blade up off of the bed and carrying it like a child to where I stood. "I need you to cut me. To let me start over."

I took the blade, if only to stop her speaking. "I can't do that, Tengi," I whispered. "I couldn't. Not to anyone."

Tengi nodded but did not move. "I know how it sounds, but look at me. Look at what has become of me, Mina." For the first time she looked at me closely, her eyes on my hidden memories. "Look what's happened to you!" Her voice bounced around my room and I held my finger to her lips.

"My father," I whispered.

She batted my hand like a fly. "We have been destroyed by the acts of others. Two people locked my door and held me down and made me remember something I want to forget. Why should *I* have to remember what *they* did? Why should you have to hide yourself when you're alone?"

"But your mother!" I said, losing grip on my voice. "You always said she would regret this, that she was a pretender."

Tengi nodded. "She was. She didn't do it for herself. She did it so that others wouldn't think less of her. She was a coward. I'm not afraid to let go."

I stared at Tengi, her nostrils flaring, her eyes wide as a street cat. My heart swam in my ears. My grandmother would say it was cowardice, not bravery. "You aren't serious," I said. "You can't be."

Her fingers wrapped around my shoulders. Ropes of tendon sprung out on her neck. "We deserve something new. The dance is coming tomorrow. There will be so many boats lining the dock that slipping in to one will be easy. While everyone stares at the sky, their eyes filled with fireworks, we will move beneath them and climb onto the boat unseen. We'll start our new lives without *these*," Tengi shook her memories in her fists like they were chains, "weighing us down. It's the New Sun. It's the time of new beginnings."

"Not for people like me," I said. Memories of my mother flooded me. Fireworks above new-budded flowers, her breath on my scalp, her voice in my ear. Watching the lives of other people.

Tengi reached behind me, undid my knots, and I felt my memories crash around my shoulders. She found those four finger lengths, held them. They were the most precious things I possessed. Yet they were also nothing. They were not real. Not like Tengi. Not like the dagger in my hand. Not like the moon filtering through the cracks of my ceiling. Not like the cold air seeping through the floor. Not like my father dragging himself from the mattress, where I could hear him hobbling now beneath us.

Tengi placed her memory in my hand and closed her eyes. I held her and wondered which memories she would miss most. Her comfortable childhood, or the sweaty nights cramped in a room above a Helm parlor? Would she long for what she'd lost, even if she couldn't remember? Be like my father, still reaching down to scratch his missing foot? Would she lose herself? Lose her interest in me?

And who would I be without my mother's breath on my scalp, my grandmother's slap against my cheek? I thought of the fireworks, the fractals, the poppies. *One day you will have memories like that.*

"Take all but right now," said Tengi, her breath hot against my face. "I don't want to remember anything but us and our plan for the boats. I've written down all we need to remember."

I felt my body vibrate. I did not move.

"We can meet again. That will be our first memory." And then Tengi pressed her lips against my scalp, my damage, so that they came to me like a memory and a moment all at once.

We are silent as we listen to my father's halting steps beneath, hear his hoarse voice calling: "Mina?" It will take him some time to climb to my room. To find our spirits entwined. It will take him only moments to understand when he opens my door. To step his way into my room in the eclipsed moonlight, to find my past dead on the ground. Find my life spread out in tight curls at his feet. Find me taken up by a longed-for breeze, flying around the room. He will pass the moths heading for the flames through my open window, intent on breaking through the glass of the lamp to experience the moment they have lived for, that they will die for. He will hear familiar nervous laughter and confused footsteps pattering on the walking boards outside. He will peer out into the inky dark, the moon now lost behind the Tower, and will try to find me. He will see instead two strangers, their hands clasped, bouncing as if unmoored and drifting from a dock. Watch them feeling in the black for the way forward.

"See Nicholas M. Stillman's story "The Memory Dresser" online at Metaphorosis.
If you liked it, leave a comment. Authors love that!
Remember to subscribe to our e-mail updates so you'll know when new stories are posted."

About the story

This story started, like most stories, with an observation. I was sitting in bed with my then-wife, and she was holding out her hair to me, clipped off like held by imaginary scissors.

I want to get my hair cut to here, she said. Her eyes pinched and she looked closely at the strands. But it's hard. Think of all the things that this hair has been through.

I nodded. Then nodded more emphatically as I felt that familiar euphoria that writers feel when their story brain, constantly scanning for entries, unearths something tantalizing.

That's a story, I said.

How? she said.

I don't know, I said.

It stayed an idea until my then-wife left, thus bridging the distance between then and now. The absence was like removing a limb. I felt keenly that I had lost part of myself, that half of my collective memories from the last decade had suddenly vanished. That feeling of loss at not only losing someone but losing your own past was the impetus for the first drafts of "The Memory Dresser." Of course, *Eternal Sunshine of the Spotless Mind* already existed, though I hadn't yet seen it.

It was later, while reading Frank Herbert's *Dune*, that I decided to build a world where memory is malleable, external, and able to be hidden. The possibilities for stories in a world like that felt endless.

The first draft of that story garnered me an acceptance into an MFA program. The second and third netted me rejections from magazines, but with it a feeling of progress. I was getting closer to something I considered true, but still hadn't reached.

The characters of Mina and Tengi had been in the drafts for so long that I took for granted the power of their emotional conflicts. In this latest version, I wanted to capture the disparate feelings of pretending to have had a great past and not feeling the need to reveal trauma to the world. I wanted to investigate the differences between coping, hiding, and repressing, and physicalize them in a fantasy setting where I felt I could better wrestle with them.

As I evolved my understanding of the connection between how we present ourselves to the world and how we choose to define that presentation, the final scene's ethical implications evolved as well. The decision to cut all the memories no longer felt heroic to me, as it did in the earliest draft. Is eliminating your past an ethical way to handle trauma? Is there a "proper" way? The characters had made their decision, but I had still had questions and wanted to follow them to see how it turned out. Like them, I'm still feeling in the dark from what comes next.

A question for the author

Q: What is the hardest part of writing for you?

A: Is The Entirety of the Revision Process an acceptable response?

I was famous in my workshops for being a "Blank Page Reviser," meaning I stripped my stories down to nothing when even the fewest amount of revisions were suggested. Even this story, "The Memory Dresser," has been rewritten from a blank page at least five times. I thought this strategy demonstrated my dedication, my perfectionism, and a mind brimming with new ideas. While all of those might be true, I feel it also speaks to a deeper truth: revision requires an objective form of self-analysis which is difficult to practice. It means knowing the difference between writing a bad scene and having low self-esteem, or a good scene and an inflated ego.

I think a lot about the Dunning-Kruger Effect, or: "the more you know, the more you know you don't know." For me, this is the crux of the paradox of revising. The more I write, the more keenly aware of my writing deficiencies I become, the less confident my writing becomes, the worse it gets. Essentially, my self-confidence was much higher when I was much worse. This, I don't think, is fair.

And so I tinker, I dabble, I erase, I re-write and the more I do it, the worse I feel. Yet, here I am. Bulldozing and sawing and reimagining a perfectly acceptable painting of a shed until it looks like a boat, which is not better or worse—just different. Have you seen my boat? I ask. What happened to the shed? they ask. One moment, I say as I begin painting for them a fresh pterodactyl.

But, occasionally, in a moment of unexpected glory, I realize that the pterodactyl, not the shed or the boat, was what I had been trying for so long to create.

About the author

Nicholas M. Stillman is a writer, teacher, and reluctant service worker living in the east bay in California. He received his MFA from Saint Mary's College of California in 2018, where he currently teaches English. He desperately wants to live in the woods, raise crops, write eight hours a day, and play an unhealthy amount of PS4. He shares this impossible dream with his girlfriend, Sabrina, and their cats, Gnocchi and Fusilli, who all insisted on being part of this bio.

@nick_at_day

Unmasked

Tomas Marcantonio

There isn't much difference between night and day in this city, but we know it must be night when the train comes. It stops in the centre of the city inside its glass tube, the passengers standing shoulder to shoulder with their faces at the window: The Rat, The Flamingo, The Impala, several more, all of them watching us. After an hour or so the train moves on, out through the wall that encircles the city. In through one wall and out the other, like one of those underwater tunnels in aquariums.

When the train disappears, I'm left as always with the afterimage of The Donkey.

Most of the figures on the train don't bother me, but when I look through The Donkey's mask I can see something of the lights in her eyes. I feel the weight of her gaze in my every movement, see flashes in the black recesses of my mind, like the blink of a lighthouse seen from way out at sea.

Yu-na and I stand outside the mess hall and wait for the siren. Yu-na's chewing absently on the silky black hair that falls past her cheeks; a habit I've tried endlessly to get her to break. I run a hand across her cheek and gently pluck the hair from her lips, and she fixes me with a stare that's devoid of emotion. Every time I look at her, I wonder how two young women could look more different. Yu-na's skin is pale and translucent, her nose petite and perfectly formed, her curves womanly and in proportion. I stand opposite her with my shaved head, my boyish limbs that look too long for my body, the holes in my ears and nose, the ones I presume were left by piercings in my old life.

Yu-na's hand is cold within mine, but her grip is firm, as though she fears she might float away if she let go. With this thought, I instinctively look towards the metal ceiling of the city, and remember there's nowhere to float away to.

Yu-na closes her eyes and tears form on the tips of her lashes; I know what's going to happen but there's nothing I can do about it. She drops suddenly to her knees, drops her chin onto her chest, and her whole body starts to shake. I wrap an arm around her shoulders, try to calm her. It doesn't help, but it's all I can think to do. The panic attacks have been getting worse for weeks but the medic only tells us there's nothing wrong; whatever it is, it's all in her head. When the shaking stops, I cradle Yu-na in my arms.

The siren doesn't come. "No one's being taken tonight," I say into her ear.

I slide one finger across Yu-na's cheeks to wipe away the worst of the tears, pull her to her feet. All I want now is a drink, but first I have to get Yu-na back to the residences. We head east and are swallowed by the backstreets of The Web, a network of labyrinthine alleyways. All of them are glazed in blinking neon, as though a giant cat with fluorescent nails has claimed the walls as scratching posts. Smoke spills out of the back windows, the red lights of cameras flash on the cracked-mortar walls, the gutters exude the sour stench of human waste. None of us remember where we lived before; we remember the reunification, the wars, the names of cities – Seoul, Busan, Daegu – but that's all they are: names. For all of us, though, there's something familiar about these alleys, these neon signs. Just like we know that there were cars, jobs, families somewhere in our past lives, we know that these neon-lit arteries are a piece of home.

A couple of red-faced young women are on their haunches outside the back door of one of the kitchens; they eyeball us silently as we make for the underpass beneath the train tracks. We hold our breaths to block out the smell of piss and pass a drunk leaning up against one wall. He detaches himself from the brown brick and stumbles our way, his red-veined eyes trained on both of us. Yu-na scrunches her eyes shut; another one of her attacks is coming. I position myself between her and him.

"Another step and I'll spread your nose all over your face," I tell him.

He just laughs and hiccups. I shove him backwards against the wall and shepherd Yu-na quickly through to the other side of the underpass.

We're halfway across the square when the siren sounds. I swear under my breath. A late siren: it's rare, but it happens. Yu-na and I stand stock still, looking up at the ceiling high above, waiting. Yu-na takes my hand again.

"One minute," the voice says. It's always the same voice that comes from the speakers around the city walls: a man's voice, disjointed and off-key, as though it's been put through a computer. The one minute warning is how it always starts. We all wait for the name.

"Hwang Yu-na," the voice says.

My heart drops into my stomach. Yu-na looks at me, the fear suddenly emptying her black eyes, like a pool of ink being sucked away down a drain.

"No," she whispers, and even though her voice is so quiet I can hear the way it breaks as she utters that one syllable.

"It's okay, it's okay," is all I can say, over and over again in Yu-na's ear. I just want to hold her and keep her with me. I'm certain that whatever life Yu-na had before, she's better off here with me, with her simple chores and her quiet hours alone in the library.

The second siren sounds, and that's the cue for the ceiling to open. Yu-na buries her face into my shoulder and I look up. The metal plates separate like a giant mechanical beetle opening its wings; the echoing sound is of rusted iron teeth grinding together.

The bystanders in the square form a circle a safe distance around us; we've all been told what happens when someone tries to interfere with the mosquitoes. The metal half-moons continue to slide apart, and soon enough we can see the night sky beyond them. It's black and there are no stars tonight. Yu-na is shaking in my arms. Then we see the silhouettes of the mosquitoes.

They descend slowly through the hole in the ceiling. It's a few seconds before we can make them out properly: their arms and legs and tight black clothes, the packs on their backs which drone like motorcycle engines, their masks with white eyes and elongated noses like enormous flies. There are three as always, circling downwards, ever closer.

"Don't let them take me," Yu-na whispers into my ear; her breath is like a butterfly fluttering through the air with a torn wing. The words break my heart, but I can't do anything. The mosquitoes pause just a few feet above us; they're waiting for me to move, to make their target clear. They won't wait for long.

"I won't let them touch you," I promise.

I hear something of the murmurs of the crowd around us, the restlessness of the mosquitoes above our heads. I try to block them out.

"Go," Yu-na whispers, letting me go.

I don't move. It goes against everything we've ever been taught; everyone knows what happens when you don't follow the rules, but I have no past, and Yu-na's the only thing I have in my life worth holding onto.

The mosquitoes descend and plant their feet on the ground, forming a circle around us. I hear the crowd calling for me to move, but I stand my ground as the first mosquito approaches, balling my hands into fists. He pulls out a metal stick from his belt and brandishes it in front of me. I ignore the protests and screams of the crowd and try to make a grab for it, but the shock passes up my arm on impact, electricity coursing through my very bones. I fall backwards on the floor and hold my arm until the pain ceases, and I open my eyes just in time to see the mosquitoes closing in on Yu-na, standing defenceless with her hands at her sides.

"I'll find you on the outside!" I call to her.

Then one of them makes the injection, the bite, and Yu-na falls limp into their arms. A second later they're off the ground, leaning into the sky like helicopters, Yu-na held between them. We all watch the sky until the silhouettes are beyond the open ceiling, disappearing into the black abyss. A few moments later the giant metal plates begin to slide shut again. The light hardly changes; we're still in darkness, the only patches of light coming from the artificial green glow of the mercury-vapour lamps. Gradually the square empties and I am alone, a defeated heap on the floor, looking up at the ceiling.

The next day goes by like any other. I spend the hours between eight and two with Sung-sook, a weathered fifty-something woman with a stout body and a brown, leathery face, punctured with deep-set eyes and square, yellow teeth. She's one of the Originals: here from the start, whenever that was, and never been taken. They each have their own area of expertise: fishing, carpentry, medicine, cooking, textiles, electronics. I've been with Sung-sook for two weeks already and she seems to think less of me with each passing day.

Each morning we unfurl the nets and take out one of the wooden fishing dories that we leave each night on the beach. Sung-sook and I sit on the boat half-way between the beach and the iron wall, waiting for the fish to come.

"You were a fool to interfere," she says to me, breaking our unspoken pact of silence. "They'll take you for sure tomorrow. And then there's no coming back."

I keep my eyes on the water, remembering the first time I saw it six months ago, waking up face-down in the sand with my name tag tied around my wrist. Very few stay in the city longer than I have.

At Sung-sook's command, we pull in the nets and separate the fish. The smaller ones are thrown back into the water; we take the others into one of the shacks at the top of the beach, smash their heads against the wooden table and gut them. Sung-sook criticises my technique, tells me I'm too impatient, her nostrils flaring and contracting like a racehorse before the starting gate. I bite my tongue and wait for her to dismiss me, and I go back to the residences to shower and scrub my hands to try to lose the smell of fish guts. I still have some of Yuna's alcohol vouchers from last week. Tonight I'm going to use them all.

I've already used up my restaurant passes for the month, so once again I've got the basic dinner – rice with a few side dishes: kimchi, bean sprouts, spinach; whatever gets delivered each week from the sky. I'm filing out of the mess hall with a few others when the train arrives. It comes with no sound, as usual; it just rolls slowly into the city and stops just beyond the square. Usually I try to avoid looking at the masked figures inside, but I see the train windows in my peripheral vision, and I know straight away that something's not right.

I walk over towards the glass tube, scanning the windows of the three carriages. I'm not the only one to have noticed; others nearby are also making their way to the train for a closer look. The windows are empty; the masked figures are gone. Sung-sook is behind me, breathing heavily through her nose like a bull.

"Stay back," she barks at the approaching crowd, but no one listens.

I'm only a few feet away when I see that the train isn't empty at all. I see the masked figures through the glass doors, lying on the carriage floors in pools of red.

Some onlookers put their hands over their mouths. Others are looking up to the ceiling as though waiting for it to open, for the mosquitoes to come down and offer an explanation.

Then the doors begin to open. First the doors to the glass tunnel, then the doors to the train itself. For the first time ever.

We all instinctively look to the Originals in the crowd, but they seem as clueless as the rest of us. This has never happened before; we weren't given guidelines on this. The doors aren't *supposed* to open.

Then a voice.

"Doors closing. Five."

We all look at each other, wondering if we should let this one chance slip away from us. If the doors close, the train will pass on through the city like it always does, and we might never see it again.

"Four."

Perhaps if the masked figures are dead, the people who give us our supplies are dead, too. Perhaps we'll be left here forever; no mosquitoes, no supplies, left to rot beneath the iron ceiling above us.

"Three."

Perhaps if we get on the train we'll be taken directly to whoever killed these people. We could be going right into the hands of death.

"Two."

But this might be my only chance to find Yu-na. To hold her, tell her everything will be all right. I promised her, and I never thought I'd actually have the chance to keep it. I know it probably won't come again.

"One."

No one's moving. Only me.

Sung-sook sees what I'm about to do before anyone else, but she's too slow. Her stout fingers clutch at my shirt, but I shake myself free and squeeze through the doors just as they're closing. I'm aboard, standing between the fallen bodies, and the glass tunnel doors close behind me. Sung-sook watches me with her big cow eyes, and for the first time I see something like concern in them. The train begins to move.

The eyes in the masks are empty and black. The Impala's body is twisted awkwardly; it looks like her neck has been broken. The Owl has three bullet holes in his chest. The others are all splayed out in different positions, like an exhibit of the various shapes of death. I drop to my haunches and reach for the mask of The Flamingo. The face beneath is human; a young man, his eyes closed, his tongue hanging grotesquely out of his mouth. I check his pulse, examine the wounds on his body. He's dead, unmistakably. They're all dead. The only one I can't see is The Donkey.

The train is almost at the city limits. For the first time, at least for the first time that I can remember, I'm going to see what's outside this city. When it reaches the rusting iron wall, the carriage plunges into darkness. For several seconds, that's all there is. Then the train stops.

The doors open, and silver light spills into the carriage. I step off the train onto a platform and find myself inside an empty station no bigger than one of the residences. There's nothing apart from four grey walls, a ceiling punctuated by fluorescent lamps, and a metal door across from the tracks. I stand in front of it for a few seconds. Then I push it open, and just like that I'm free.

I'm under the open sky. It's a sky full of stars with just a few patches of cloud. The smell of the open air fills my nostrils and in that split second I'm sure I can remember everything about my past life. But as quickly as the memory came, it disappears, like a candle that's snuffed out before the flame has had a chance to breathe and take form.

I'm in a valley surrounded by high blue mountains. There's grass under my feet; fields spread out before me, and a dark, still lake. There's no one else here. There's no one to tell me where to go, what to do. I could run for the mountains and see where they take me. But I can't. I think of all the people still trapped in the city. More importantly, I can't just leave without finding the answers. Where Yu-na was taken. Who took her. Who did this to us.

To my right is the city and the train station. It only occurs to me now that the tracks go no further; the train simply shuttles in and out of the city, like a toy engine being rolled back and forth along the carpet by a child. A giant, translucent dome stands about two hundred yards to my left, resembling a giant greenhouse. The only other building in the valley is smaller; it's one-storey, made of concrete, with an aluminium roof and a steel door.

I push it open. The corridor in front of me is dark and has a distinctive chemical smell. Naked light bulbs illuminate the hallway and its doors from the ceiling, but many of them are flashing wildly as if they're about to pop, and I'm forced to shield my eyes and squint.

I try the first doors on either side; an empty boardroom, then an office, full of computers and screens; everything is switched off. Then a store room, stocked with bags of rice, boxes of other supplies. Along the back wall are the animal masks, hanging up like a hunter's trophies. Next to them are the rubber gas masks of the mosquitoes; the metal tanks of their jet-packs are in a pile in the corner.

The next door along has a sign on it: Records. The room is filled with cabinets, drawers, the names on their labels organised in alphabetical order: Kang Jong-woo, Kang Hye-jin, Ko Jae-kwon. I pull open a couple; they're full of folders, documents. I follow the line, reading every name, some of which I recognise from the city. I skip ahead through the Kims and Moons and Parks until I find myself: Yoo Min-soo.

I pull out one of my folders with my hands shaking. I find photos of myself; photos of others with dates and fact files and paragraphs detailing their relationships with me. Distant relatives, friends, ex-boyfriends. I look into each of their faces but they mean nothing to me. If these people were ever a part of my life, I don't remember them.

Then I see a man and a woman in their forties, with plain faces and neutral expressions. I recognise my likeness in each of them; I have my mother's wide nose and my father's thick eyebrows, but I remember nothing about them. I stare at the photos, I don't know for how long, wondering if these people know where I am right now, whether they lay awake at night unable to sleep, wondering what happened to their daughter.

The next folder is marked 'Criminal Activity and Sentencing'. I read the first page with my heart throbbing so hard I can barely hear myself think.

Yoo Min-soo, 18, was arrested on the 3rd September 2036 for the murder of her father, Yoo Jong-min. The victim was found dead on his donkey farm just outside of Busan with fourteen stab wounds. Yoo Min-soo later came forward and confessed to her father's murder. She claimed that the attack was retribution for her father's attack on his wife, Seo Hyeon-mi, which left her in a coma.

Yoo Min-soo had previously shown no prior tendency for violence. She has been described by classmates and teachers as an aloof but normal teenager. All of the character witnesses described the murder as being out of character.

Yoo Min-soo was initially sentenced to twenty years in prison. Having served four months of her prison term, Min-soo was selected for the Future Justice Project after careful consideration by the board of trustees. She accepted the offer on 7th January 2037 and was transported to the company's headquarters the next morning. Her statement before entering the facility, included in full on the following page, cites the condition of her mother, who remains comatose, and the traumatic memories of the murder of her father as being the main *incentives for accepting the invitation to the project.*

I drop the folder. I feel dizzy and sick. For a few moments I'm sure that I'm going to vomit. I double up and lean against the cabinets, trying to control my breathing. I don't remember any of it. I don't remember my father, I don't remember killing him. That was all someone else. But whatever the city and the Future Justice Project are all about, it looks like my past self agreed to it.

I leave the drawer open and the papers on the floor and stumble outside the room. Back out in the corridor, the lights are still flickering above me, but there's no other movement. The door at the end of the corridor is ajar, and the lights are on inside. I head straight for it and push the door open, finding myself in a room that resembles a small hospital ward. The first thing I see is Yu-na, lying on a bed with white sheets tucked tightly around her, her eyes closed.

"Yu-na!" I call, shaking her. "Wake up!"

She doesn't move.

"She might not wake up for a little while."

The voice makes me jump. There's a tall woman in a white coat standing behind me. She's in her thirties, her black hair tied back in a ponytail. Her face has a grey pallor and her eyes are glassy.

"Min-soo," she says. There's no hint of surprise in her voice. "Did anyone else get on the train?"

I shake my head.

The woman's eyes are unfocused, wide; they move slowly, taking in nothing. She steps past me like a ghost and lowers herself heavily into the chair next to Yuna's bed.

"What happened in there?" I ask. "The people on the train."

"They were the scientists," she says, staring at a spot on the floor.

I look around the room. There are three other beds, all empty, surrounded by monitors and medical equipment on trays.

"What happened to them?"

The woman doesn't answer.

"I read my file," I say. The woman nods. I want her to tell me that none of it is true, that it's a mistake, but she says nothing. "Where are we?" I ask. "That big dome out there..."

The woman slowly looks up at me, with more clarity this time. "That was Site 1. From the project's early days. It was thriving then, or at least that's what we all believed."

"What happened?"

The woman takes a breath. "One of the criminals re-offended a couple of years after his release. Of course, many people wanted to shut the project down after that. But three years later the government decided to give it one more chance, with new conditions, of course. That's when they moved to Site 2, the one you've been living in this past six months. No sky, no fresh air, the intimidating figures on the train. And the mosquitoes, of course, as you call them. It was thought that these elements would stimulate your aggressive natures, provide a better platform for the tests."

"The tests. What are they?"

"Nothing new," the woman says dismissively. "Psychological questions, behavioural tests. Workplaces have been using them for years to identify potentially dangerous individuals. Really, those tests are just a formality. Your real test is what happens in the compound. They watch and analyse everything, monitor every discussion, every drunken argument. They wanted to see what would happen when you were relieved of your traumatic memories. To see if you posed any threat to society without them."

I look at Yu-na's face, peaceful in sleep. "Did she pass?"

"She did; her original sentence has been revoked. Of course, they always expected her to. Yu-na's exactly the kind of person the project was created for: victims of unfavourable upbringings, violent acts. That's what the Future Justice Project was all about: seeking out criminals who were victims themselves; people who were traumatized, who would have lived normal lives if it weren't for another person's evil."

"What happened to her?"

The woman looks at me as though to judge whether I can take it. She takes another deep, shaking breath before answering.

"A man tried to force himself on her one night in Seoul. Forced her into an alleyway, put his hand over her mouth."

I look at my friend again. I think about her panic attacks.

"Yu-na killed him," I say.

The woman nods. "She tracked him down a few nights after the attack. Stabbed him. She's recovering now from her memory wipe. She was due to leave tomorrow morning, to re-enter society with a clean slate, start her new life."

I look at the woman.

"Why do you keep saying 'they'?" I ask. "You're one of them, aren't you? The ones who were watching us? The scientists?"

She stares at the floor again. "I really expected more than one person to get on the train," she says, almost to herself. "Thought that I could blame it on all of you, escaping, taking your revenge." She smiles ruefully. "I couldn't even get that part right."

Her eyes are changing again. They lose their focus, flitting around the room until eventually settling on Yu-na's sleeping face.

"Yu-na and I have a lot in common, you know," she says, putting a hand on Yu-na's pale cheek. "Although Yu-na fought her attacker off, so I suppose you could say she was luckier than I was."

I notice the way her hands shake, the nervous countenance of her eyes, and I start to take stock of the room. There's nothing close at hand; only the tray of instruments next to Yu-na's bed.

"The criminal who was released from Site 1," she continues, looking at Yu-na's closed eyes as though reading a bedtime story to a sleeping child. "He went to a small village near Gyeongju to start his new life. It was there that he assaulted a young woman who worked for the government."

"So you're not a scientist," I say, edging slowly towards the tray. If only I can grab one of the needles. "You work for the government."

"We're rather far from civilisation out here," the woman goes on. "Someone had to stay here and make sure the government's guidelines were being followed, report on developments. Who better to judge the project than the victim of one of its failures? I suppose they thought I might provide a contrasting viewpoint."

She sighs and appeals to Yu-na with a weak smile. I'm at the foot of the bed now. Just a little further.

"The oldest debate in the book, isn't it?" she says, still looking into Yu-na's face. "Nature versus nurture. But who are therapists and psychologists to say whether prison is deserved or not? Can we really just let criminals waltz back into cities as if they've done nothing wrong?"

She looks up at me now as though imploring me to find an answer. I stop inching forwards but say nothing.

"I haven't felt safe since the night it happened all those years ago," the woman goes on. "I'll probably never feel safe. Do you understand that?"

"You killed them," I say, looking directly into her eyes. "A dozen at least. You're as bad as every single person living in that city. Probably even worse."

Her eyes are shining now; tears are collecting on her lashes.

"I thought it was the only way to end it," she says, shaking her head as the tears trickle down her cheeks. "I thought their deaths would save so many more in the long run."

She puts her head in her hands and sits there, shaking, tears dribbling through her fingers and down her wrists. I take my chance, reaching for the closest needle; I hold it in one hand, raise it aloft.

She looks up and sees what I'm about to do. There's no fear in her eyes, only regret and resignation.

"Let me just ask you one thing, Min-soo." She stands up. "Do you really think you would have passed your test?"

I hold the needle in position.

"I saw the drone footage from that day. On your father's farm, when you found your mother lying there unconscious. You ran out from the kitchen and attacked him, right there in the middle of one of the animal enclosures. I'll never forget that look in your eyes; it was barely human. And the sound of the beasts, that was almost worse than the sight of the blood. Even they recognised the horror of what you were doing. I never thought for a minute that I could do something like that. But I did."

Now I know for sure that it's her. I remember the shape of her body, the look in her eyes. The Donkey, standing right in front of me.

"The mask," I say.

She nods, but her eyes have glassed over again. "We thought it might stir something, somewhere in the depths of your mind. Bring about a reaction in one way or another. We did it with several others, too, of course. The scientists were always against it, but the government felt that after Site 1 failed, any extra intimidation would be useful."

At that moment Yu-na's eyes open. She blinks slowly, trying to bring the room into focus.

The Donkey hardly reacts; she seems only half-present, as though part of her soul has absconded to another room. I drop the needle, spring to Yu-na's side and take her hand. She pulls herself up on the bed, but it's clear that she has no idea who I am. She's starting all over again.

"Headquarters," The Donkey says, again almost to herself. "In Seoul. They'll be in contact soon."

She's pulling something slowly out of the back of her trousers. Yu-na screams at the sight of the gun and scrambles off the bed onto the floor, backing away behind me on her hands and knees. I hold my hands up and step around the bed towards The Donkey.

"You don't have to do this," I say. "You can let us go. No one has to know."

The Donkey just stares at the gun, as though seeing it for the first time.

I don't know what to say to stop her. Part of me thinks that it doesn't matter whether I live or die anyway. I have no memory; no friends, no family, no place to call a home. I'm an empty shell, but I'm still a murderer. Maybe this woman's right to get rid of me.

But then I look at Yu-na, now cowering at my back. She doesn't know who I am, or what promise I made to her, but I know her. I know what she did and why, and for all I know she's the only person I've ever truly cared about. Even if I don't deserve to go on living, she does.

I turn back to The Donkey.

"We're all tested," I say to her. "And you're right, I don't know if I would've passed mine. There's something in me that I might not be able to control. They might not have seen it on those cameras, but I feel it sometimes. And you know what, if I had the chance to kill my father again, if he did what the file says, I'd probably do it. Maybe I'd fail my test, but you don't have to fail yours. We can fix this. You can do the right thing."

The Donkey might be listening, but she's not looking at me. She's looking over my shoulder at Yu-na.

"You don't remember it, do you?" she asks Yu-na.

Behind me, Yu-na buries her face in my shoulder.

"You don't remember how it feels, but I do." She looks up at the ceiling, blinking away tears. "I'll live with that memory forever. And now I'll live with their deaths, too. You're right, Min-soo," she adds, looking at me. "I'm worse than all of you. This is my test."

She looks back to the gun, shaking in her hands.

"This is my test," The Donkey says again, more quietly, her face distorted. "And I've failed it."

She moves the gun slowly towards her temple, but I spring forward and wrestle it from her before she can pull the trigger. I pin her to the ground.

"No," I tell her. "It doesn't have to be that way. Show me how to do the memory wipe. Show me, and you can be rid of it all."

"You can leave if you want," I tell the crowded square. I'm standing in front of all of them beneath the metal ceiling of the city, Yu-na and The Donkey at my side, looking passively over the crowd. "But we're staying. Outside these walls is another site where we can grow our own food. Between this city and Site 1 and the resources in the valley, we can make a new life, be self-sufficient."

I look at the faces in front of me. Sung-sook is there at the front, her jaw grinding as she listens, like a cow chewing on the cud of my words.

"It might be weeks before they come, but they'll come eventually, and I don't know what will happen when they do. Maybe they'll put an end to the project altogether, put us back in prison. Maybe they'll let us return to the outside world. Or maybe they'll see that we can live in peace if we're left alone.

"I say we burn the files; those lives are over, and no one here needs to know what they've done. It won't help, it won't make you remember. It will only make things worse.

"You're free to make your own choice, but all I can tell you for certain is that the world out there won't be any kinder to you than the one we can create here. We agreed to this; all of us did. There's not a person here who can go back to a loving family; there's not a person here who wasn't wronged, who wasn't traumatized.

"We've been given a second chance, and now we can take it. This is our test."

I look at the faces in the crowd again; a few heads are nodding. None of them know what crimes they've committed;

none of them know their pasts. I'm the
only one. I'm the only one who knows the
monster lurking within myself. Even as I
speak, I can hear the braying of the
donkeys on the farm. I imagine a dead-
eyed version of myself stabbing my own
father, again and again.

I feel the weight of the gun that's
tucked into the back of my jeans. Even
after everything I've said, I can't help
wondering if The Donkey was right all
along. Who's to say that we deserve
forgiveness? Who's to say that we
shouldn't be punished for what we've
done? Are the faces in front of me truly
empty shells, as mindless and grotesque
as the animal masks hanging up on the
wall? Are those monsters within us
extracted with the memories, or are they
lurking there, biding their time, waiting
for the right moment to burst forth?

I finger the photograph in my pocket,
the one of my mother. All I know about
her is that she's lying in a hospital bed
somewhere, as empty as I am. But I chose
to leave her; to forget, so that I could have
a fresh start. That's who I am. That's who
I am beneath the mask.

Yu-na takes my hand. She doesn't
smile, but I'm used to that. Her memories

have been wiped, but nothing about her seems to have changed. She's still the girl I'd do anything to keep from being parted from. I won't make the same mistake again; I won't let go of someone I love. A few strands of silky hair pass across her cheek and she pulls them into her mouth with her tongue, like a frog casually catching a passing fly. She chews on her hair, just as she's done every day since I've known her.

See Tomas Marcantonio's story "Unmasked" online at Metaphorosis.
If you liked it, leave a comment. Authors love that!
Remember to subscribe to our e-mail updates so you'll know when new stories are posted.

About the story

I've always enjoyed reading about dystopian societies, especially ones where the main characters are in the dark about their pasts or the nature of their worlds. The set-up and slow uncovering of the truth is usually the highlight of these stories, but I wanted to write something that challenged the reader even after the "grand reveal".

Min-soo, the protagonist of "Unmasked", spends six months inside a walled, roofed city before she uncovers the truth of why she and all the other inhabitants are there. When she does, things aren't tied up neatly in bows; this story deals with difficult questions regarding crime and punishment, and the age-old debate of nature versus nurture.

Hopefully the reader sympathises with the main characters in the story, but at the same time they won't come away thinking of them as heroes. The story's key concept is a controversial one and there's no clear good or evil, and no clear right or wrong. My aim with this "Unmasked" was to get the reader thinking, and I'm pleased with how it turned out.

A question for the author

Q: What is your favorite fairy tale and why?

A: Beauty and the Beast. A wonderful romance, but also because the Beast's library is to die for.

About the author

Tomas Marcantonio is a fiction and travel writer based in Busan, South Korea. He splits his time between teaching, writing, and getting lost in neon-lit backstreets.

@TJMarcantonio

Copyright

Metaphorosis Publishing

Metaphorosis offers beautifully written science fiction and fantasy. Our projects include:

Metaphorosis Magazine

Metaphorosis, a weekly magazine of SFF short stories, including stories from all the authors in this anthology. Find out more at magazine.metaphorosis.com, and sign up to be notified of new stories.

Metaphorosis Books

Recent books from Metaphorosis can be found at <u>books.metaphorosis.com</u>, and include:

Score

an SFF symphony

What if stories were written like music? *Score* is an anthology of stories written to an emotional score.

Best Vegan SFF of 2018

The best vegan science fiction and fantasy stories of 2018!

Metaphorosis 2018

Metaphorosis: Best of 2018

All the stories from *Metaphorosis* magazine's third year. Fifty-two great SFF stories.

The best science fiction and fantasy stories from *Metaphorosis* magazine's third year.

Metaphorosis 2017

Metaphorosis: Best of 2017

All the stories from *Metaphorosis* magazine's second year. Fifty-three great SFF stories.

The best science fiction and fantasy stories from *Metaphorosis* magazine's *second* year.

**Metaphorosis
2016**

Almost all the
stories from
Metaphorosis
magazine's first
year.

**Metaphorosis:
Best of 2016**

The best science
fiction and fantasy
stories from
Metaphorosis
magazine's first
year.

Reading 5X5

Five stories, five times

Twenty-five SFF authors, five base stories, five versions of each – see how different writers take on the same material, with stories in contemporary and high fantasy, soft and hard SF, and a mysterious 'other' category.

Reading 5X5

Writers' Edition

All the stories from the regular, readers' edition, plus two extra stories, the story seed, and authors' notes on writing. Over 100 pages of additional material specifically aimed at writers.

Best Vegan SFF of 2017

The best vegan science fiction and fantasy stories of 2017!

Best Vegan SFF of 2016

The best vegan science fiction and fantasy stories of 2016!

Susurrus

A darkly romantic story of magic, love, and suffering.